THE LIBRARY DETECTIVE

Hal Johnson is a retired cop who works for his city's public library, tracking down missing and overdue books. But his switch of careers is no sinecure, for his work always seems to lead him into some sort of mystery, such as blackmail, robbery, kidnapping — and even murder. In the course of collecting fines and recovering books, Hal finds himself in plenty of dangerous situations that require him to use all his former police skills . . .

JAMES HOLDING

THE LIBRARY DETECTIVE

Complete and Unabridged

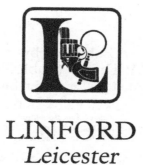

LINFORD
Leicester

First published in Great Britain

First Linford Edition
published 2017

A catalogue record for this book is available
from the British Library.

ISBN 978–1–4448–3419–2

Published by
F. A. Thorpe (Publishing)
Anstey, Leicestershire

Set by Words & Graphics Ltd.
Anstey, Leicestershire
Printed and bound in Great Britain by
T. J. International Ltd., Padstow, Cornwall

This book is printed on acid-free paper

1

Library Fuzz

It was on the north side in a shabby neighborhood six blocks off the interstate highway — one of those yellow-brick apartment houses that 60 years of grime and weather had turned to a dirty taupe.

The rank of mailboxes inside told me that Hatfield's apartment was Number 35, on the third floor. I walked up. The stairway was littered with candy wrappers, empty beer cans, and a lot of caked-on dirt. It smelled pretty ripe, too.

On the third landing I went over to the door of apartment 35 and put a finger on the buzzer. I could hear it ring inside the apartment, too loud. I looked down and saw that the door was open half an inch, unlatched, the lock twisted out of shape.

I waited for somebody to answer my ring, but nobody did. So I put an eye to the door crack and looked inside. All I got was a narrow view of a tiny foyer with two doors leading off it, both closed. I rang the bell again in case Hatfield hadn't heard it the first time. Still nothing happened.

The uneasiness that had driven me all the way out here from the public library was more than uneasiness now. My stomach was churning gently, the way it does when I'm hung over — or scared. I pushed the door wide open and said in a tentative voice, 'Hello! Anybody home? Mr. Hatfield?'

No answer. I looked at my watch and noted that the time was 9:32. Then I did what I shouldn't have done. I opened the right-hand door that led off Hatfield's foyer into a small poorly furnished living room, and there was Hatfield in front of me.

At least, I assumed it was Hatfield. I'd never met him, so I couldn't be sure. This was a slight balding man with a fringe of gray hair. He was dressed in a neat but shiny blue suit with narrow lapels. I knew the suit's lapels were narrow because one of them was visible to me from where I stood in the doorway. The other was crushed under Hatfield's body, which lay sprawled on its side on the threadbare carpet just inside the living-room door.

I sucked in my breath and held it until my stomach settled down a little. Then I stepped around Hatfield's outflung arms to get a better look at him.

There wasn't any blood that I could see. Looked as though he'd fallen while coming into the living room from the foyer. Maybe a heart attack had hit him at just that instant, I thought. It was a possibility. But not a very good one. For when I knelt beside Hatfield and felt for a pulse in his neck, I saw that the left side of his head, the side pressed against the carpet, had been caved in by a massive blow. There was blood, after all, but not much.

I stood up, feeling sick, and looked around the living room. I noticed that the toe of one of Hatfield's black loafers was snagged in a hole in the worn carpet and that a heavy fumed-oak table was perfectly positioned along the left wall of the room to have caught Hatfield's head squarely on its corner as he tripped and fell forward into the room. A quick queasy look at the corner of the table showed me more blood.

Under the edge of the table on the floor, where they must have fallen when Hatfield threw out his arms to catch himself, was a copy of yesterday's evening newspaper and a book from the public library. I could read the title of the book. *The Sound of Singing.*

I thought about that for a moment or two and decided I was pretty much out of my depth here. So I called the police. Which, even to me, seemed a rather odd thing to do — because I'm a cop myself.

★　★　★

A 'sissy' kind of a cop, it's true, but definitely a cop. And it isn't a bad job. For one thing, I don't have to carry a gun. My arrests are usually made without much fuss and never with any violence. I get a fair salary if you consider ten thousand a year a fair salary. And nobody calls me a pig, even though I am fuzz.

4

Library fuzz. What I do is chase down stolen and overdue books for the public library. Most of my work is routine and unexciting — but every once in a while I run into something that adds pepper to an otherwise bland diet.

Like this Hatfield thing.

The day before I found Hatfield's body had started off for me like any other Monday. I had a list of names and addresses to call on. Understand, the library sends out notices to book borrowers when their books are overdue; but some people are deadbeats, some are book lovers, and some are so absent-minded that they ignore the notices and hang on to the books. It's these hardcore overdues that I call on — to get the books back for the library and collect the fines owing on them.

Yesterday the first name on my list was Mrs. William Conway at an address on Sanford Street. I parked my car in the driveway of the small Cape Cod house that had the name 'Conway' on its mailbox and went up to the front door and rang the bell.

The woman who answered the door wasn't the maid, because she was dressed in a sexy nightie with a lacy robe of some sort thrown over it, and she gave me a warm, spontaneous, friendly smile before she even knew who I was. She was medium-tall in her pink bedroom slippers and had very dark hair, caught back in a ponytail by a blue ribbon, and china-blue eyes that looked almost startling under her dark eyebrows. I also noticed that she was exceptionally well put together.

What a nice way to start the day, I thought to myself. I said, 'Are you Mrs. Conway?'

'Yes,' she said, giving me a straight untroubled look with those blue eyes.

'I'm from the public library. I've come about those overdue books you have.' I showed her my identification card.

'Oh, my goodness!' she said, and her look of inquiry turned to one of stricken guilt. 'Oh, yes. Come in, won't you, Mr. Johnson? I'm really embarrassed about those books. I know I should've returned them a long time ago — I got the notices, of course. But honestly, I've been so busy!' She stepped back in mild confusion and I went into her house.

It turned out to be as unpretentious as it had looked from outside. In fact, the furnishings displayed an almost spectacular lack of taste. Well, nobody's perfect, I reminded myself. I could easily forgive Mrs. Conway's manifest ignorance of decorating principles, since she was so very decorative herself.

She switched off a color TV set that was muttering in one corner of the living room and motioned me to a chair. 'Won't you sit down?' she said tentatively. She wasn't sure just how she ought to treat a library cop.

I said politely, 'No, thanks. If you'll just give me your overdue books and the fines you owe, I'll be on my way.'

She made a little rush for a coffee table across the room, the hem of her robe swishing after her. 'I have the books right here.' She scooped up a pile of books from the table. 'I have them all ready to bring back to the library, you see?'

While I checked the book titles against my list, I asked, 'Why didn't you bring them back, Mrs. Conway?'

'My sister's been in the hospital,' she explained, 'and I've been spending every free minute with her. I just sort of forgot about my library books. I'm sorry.'

'No harm done.' I told her how much the fines amounted to and she made another little rush, this time for her purse, which hung by its strap from the back of a Windsor chair. 'The books all seem to be here,' I went on, 'except one.'

'Oh, is one missing? Which one?'

'*The Sound of Singing*.'

'That was a wonderful story!' Mrs. Conway said enthusiastically. 'Did you read it?' She sent her blue eyes around the room, searching for the missing book.

'No. But everybody seems to like it. Maybe your husband or one of the kids took it to read,' I suggested.

She gave a trill of laughter. 'I haven't any children, and my husband — ' She gestured toward a photograph of him on her desk — a dapper, youngish-looking man with a mustache and not much chin. ' — is far too busy practicing law to find time to read light novels.' She paused then, plainly puzzled.

I said gently, 'How about having a look in the other rooms, Mrs. Conway?'

'Of course.' She counted out the money for her fines and then went rushing away up the carpeted stairs to the second floor. I watched her all the way up. It was a pleasure to look at her.

In a minute she reappeared with the missing book clutched against her chest. 'Ralph *did* take it!' she said breathlessly. 'Imagine! He must have started to read it last night while I was out. It was on his bedside table under the telephone.' She handed me the book.

'Good,' I said. I took the book by its covers, pages down, and shook it — standard procedure to see if anything had been left between the pages by the borrower. You'd be surprised at what some people use to mark their places.

'I'm terribly sorry to have caused so much trouble,' Mrs. Conway said. And I knew she meant it.

I had no excuse to linger, so I took the books under my arm, said goodbye, and left, fixing Mrs. Conway's lovely face in

9

my memory alongside certain other pretty pictures I keep there to cheer me up on my low days.

I ticked off the last name on my list about one o'clock. By that time the back seat of my car was full of overdue books and my back pocket full of money for the library. Those few-cents-a-day book fines add up to a tidy sum when you put them all together, you know that? Would you believe that last year, all by myself, I collected $40,000 in fines and in the value of recovered books?

I went back to the library to turn in my day's pickings and to grab a quick lunch at the library cafeteria. About two o'clock the telephone in my closet-sized office rang, and when I answered, the switchboard girl told me there was a lady in the lobby who was asking to see me.

That surprised me. I don't get many lady visitors at the office. And the lady herself surprised me, too. She turned out to be my blue-eyed brunette of the morning, Mrs. William Conway — but a Mrs. Conway who looked as though she'd been hit in the face by a truck since I'd seen her last.

There was a bruise as big as a half-dollar on one cheek, a deep scratch on her forehead, an ugly knotted lump interrupted the smooth line of her jaw on the left side, and the flesh around one of her startling blue eyes was puffed and faintly discolored. Although she had evidently been at pains to disguise these marks with heavy make-up, they still showed. Plainly.

I suppose she saw from my expression that I'd noticed her bruises because as she sat down in my only office chair, she dropped her eyes and flushed and said with a crooked smile, 'Do I look *that* bad, Mr. Johnson?' It was a singularly beguiling gambit. Actually, battered face and all, I thought she looked just as attractive now in a lemon-colored pants suit as she had in her nightie and robe that morning.

I said, 'You look fine, Mrs. Conway.'

She tried to sound indignant. 'I fell down our stupid stairs! Can you imagine that? Just after you left. I finished making the beds and was coming down for coffee when — zap! — head over heels clear to the bottom!'

'Bad luck,' I said sympathetically, reflecting that a fall down her thickly carpeted stairs would be most unlikely to result in injuries like hers. But it was none of my business.

She said, 'What I came about, Mr. Johnson, was to see if I could get back *The Sound of Singing* you took this morning. My husband was furious when he came home for lunch and found I'd given it back to you.'

'No problem there. We must have a dozen copies of that book in — '

She interrupted me. 'Oh, but I was hoping to get the same copy I had before. You see, my husband says he left a check in it — quite a big one from a client.'

'Oh. Then I must have missed it when I shook out the book this morning.'

She nodded. 'You must have. Ralph is sure he left it there.' Mrs. Conway put a fingertip to the lump on her jaw and then hastily dropped her hand into her lap when she saw me watching her.

'Well,' I said, 'I've already turned the book back to the shelves, Mrs. Conway, but if we're lucky it'll still be in. Let me check.' I picked up my phone and asked for the librarian on the checkout desk.

Consulting my morning list of overdue book numbers, now all safely returned to circulation, I said, 'Liz, have you checked out number 15208, *The Sound of Singing*, to anybody in the last hour?'

'I've checked out that title but I don't know if it was that copy. Just a second,' Liz said. After half a minute she said, 'Yes, here it is, Hal. It went out half an hour ago on card number PC28382.'

I made a note on my desk pad of that card number, repeating the digits out loud as I did so. Then, thanking Liz, I hung up and told Mrs. Conway, 'I'm sorry, your copy's gone out again.'

'Oh, dammit anyway!' said Mrs. Conway passionately. I gathered this was pretty strong talk for her because she blushed again and threw me a distressed look before continuing. '*Everything* seems to be going wrong for me today!' She paused. 'What was that number you just took down, Mr. Johnson? Does that tell who's got the book now?'

'It tells me,' I answered. 'But for a lot of reasons we're not allowed to tell *you*. It's the card number of the person who borrowed the book.'

'Oh, dear,' she said, chewing miserably on her lower lip, 'then that's *more* bad luck, isn't it?'

I was tempted to break the library's rigid rule and give her the name and address she wanted. However, there were a couple of things besides the rule that made me restrain my chivalrous impulse. Such as no check dropping out of *The Sound of Singing* this morning when I shook the book. And such as Mrs. Conway's bruises, which looked to me more like the work of fists than of carpeted stairs.

So I said, 'I'll be glad to telephone whoever has the book now and ask him about your husband's check. Or her. If the check *is* in the book, they'll probably be glad to mail it to you.'

14

'Oh, would you, Mr. Johnson? That would be wonderful!' Her eyes lit up at once.

I called the library's main desk where they issue cards and keep the register of card holders' names and addresses. 'This is Hal Johnson,' I said. 'Look up the holder of card number PC28382 for me, will you, Kathy?'

I waited until she gave me a name — George Hatfield — and an address on the north side, then hung up, found Hatfield's telephone number in the directory, and dialed it on an outside line, feeling a little self-conscious under the anxious scrutiny of Mrs. Conway's beautiful bruised blue eye.

Nobody answered the Hatfield phone. Mrs. Conway sighed when I shook my head. 'I'll try again in an hour or so. Probably not home yet. And when I get him, I'll ask him to mail the check to you. I have your address. Okay?'

She stood up and gave me a forlorn nod. 'I guess that's the best I can do. I'll tell Ralph you're trying to get his check back, anyhow. Thanks very much.' She was still chewing on her lower lip when she left.

Later in the afternoon she called me to tell me that her husband Ralph had found his missing check in a drawer at home. There was vast relief in her voice when she told me. I wasn't relieved so much as angry — because it seemed likely to me that my beautiful Mrs. Conway had been slapped around pretty savagely by that little jerk in her photograph for a mistake she hadn't made.

Anyway, I forgot about *The Sound of Singing* and spent the rest of the afternoon shopping for a new set of belted tires for my old car.

Next morning, a few minutes before 9:00, I stopped by the library to turn in my expense voucher for the new tires and pick up my list of overdues for the day's calls. As I passed the main desk, Kathy, who was just settling down for her day's work, said, 'Hi, Hal. Stop a minute and let me see if it shows.'

I paused by the desk. 'See if what shows?'

'Senility.'

'Of course it shows, child. I'm almost forty. Why this sudden interest?'

'Only the onset of senility can account for *you* forgetting something,' Kathy said. 'The man with the famous memory.'

I was mystified. 'What did I forget?'

'The name and address of card holder PC28382, that's what. You called me to look it up for you not long after lunch yesterday, remember?'

'Sure. So what makes you think I forgot it?'

'You said you had when you called me again at four thirty for the same information.'

I stared at her. 'Me?'

She nodded. 'You.'

'I didn't call you at four thirty.'

'Somebody did. And said he was you.'

'Did it sound like my voice?'

'Certainly. An ordinary, uninteresting man's voice. Just like yours.' She grinned at me.

'Thanks. Somebody playing a joke, maybe. It wasn't me.'

While I was turning in my voucher and picking up my list of overdues, I kept thinking about Kathy's second telephone call. The more I thought about it, the more it bothered me.

So I decided to make my first call of the day on George Hatfield . . .

★   ★   ★

Well, I didn't touch anything in Hatfield's apartment until the law showed up in the persons of a uniformed patrolman and an old friend of mine, Lieutenant Randall of Homicide. I'd worked with Randall when I was in the detective bureau myself a few years back.

Randall looked at the setup in Hatfield's living room and growled, 'Why me, Hal? All you need is an ambulance on this one. The guy's had a fatal accident, that's all.'

So I told him about Mrs. Conway and her husband and *The Sound of Singing* and the mysterious telephone call to Kathy at the library. When I finished he jerked his head toward the library book lying under Hatfield's table and said, 'Is that it?'

'I haven't looked yet. I was waiting for you.'

'Look now,' Randall said. It was book number 15208, all right — unmistakably the one I'd collected yesterday from Mrs. Conway. Its identification number appeared big and clear in both the usual places — on the front flyleaf and on the margin of page 101. 'This is it. No mistake,' I said.

'If Hatfield's killing is connected with this book, as you seem to think,' Randall said reasonably enough, 'there's got to be something about the book to tell us why.'

I said, 'Maybe there was. Before the back flyleaf was torn out.'

'Be damned!' said Randall, squinting where I was pointing. 'Torn out is right. Something written on the flyleaf that this Conway wanted kept private maybe?'

'Could be.'

'Thought you said you looked through this book yesterday. You'd have seen any writing.'

'I didn't look through it. I shook it out, that's all.'

'Why would a guy write anything

private or incriminating on the blank back page of a library book, for God's sake?'

'His wife found the book under the telephone in their bedroom. He could have been taking down notes during a telephone conversation.'

'In a library book?'

'Why not, if it was the only blank paper he had handy when he got the telephone call?'

'So his wife gave the book back to you before he'd had a chance to erase his notes. Is that what you're suggesting?'

'Or transcribe them, yes. Or memorize them.'

Lieutenant Randall looked out Hatfield's grimy window for a moment. Then he said abruptly, 'I'm impounding this library book for a few days, Hal, so our lab boys can take a look at it. Okay?'

'Okay.'

Randall glanced pointedly toward the door. 'Thanks for calling us,' he said. 'Be seeing you.'

I stepped carefully around Hatfield's sprawled body. 'Right.'

'I'll be in touch if we find anything,' Randall said.

* * *

Much to my surprise he phoned me at the library just about quitting time the next day. 'Did you ever see this Mr. Conway?' he asked. 'Could you identify him?'

'I never saw him in the flesh. I saw a photo of him on his wife's desk.'

'That's good enough. Meet me at the Encore Bar at Stanhope and Cotton in twenty minutes, can you?'

'Sure,' I said. 'Why?'

'Tell you when I see you.'

He was waiting for me in a rear booth. There were only half a dozen customers in the place. I sat down facing him and he said, without preamble, 'Conway *did* write something on the back flyleaf of your library book. Or somebody did, anyhow. Because we found traces of crushed paper fibers on the page under the back flyleaf. Not good enough traces to be read except for one notation at the

21

top, which was probably written first on the back flyleaf when the pencil point was sharper and thus made a deeper groove on the page underneath. Are you with me?'

'Yes. What did it say?'

Randall got a slip of paper from his pocket and showed it to me. It contained one line, scribbled by Randall:

Transo 3212/5/13 Mi Encore Harper 6/12

I studied it silently for a minute. Randall said, faintly smug, 'Does that mean anything to you?'

'Sure,' I said, deadpan. 'Somebody named Harper off Transoceanic Airlines flight 3212 out of Miami on May 13th — that's today — is supposed to meet somebody in this bar at twelve minutes after six.'

'A lucky guess,' Randall said, crestfallen. 'The *Encore* and *Transo* gave it to you, of course. But it took us half an hour to decipher the meaning and check it out.'

'Check it out?'

'There really *is* a Transoceanic flight 3212 out of Miami today — and there really is somebody aboard named Harper, too. A Miss Genevieve Harper, stewardess.'

'Oh,' I said, 'and of course there *is* an Encore Bar — could even be a couple of them in town.'

'Only one that Harper can get to through rush-hour traffic within twenty minutes after she hits the airport,' the lieutenant said triumphantly. 'She's scheduled in at 5:52.'

I glanced at my watch. It was 5:30. 'You have time to check whether Conway had any phone calls Sunday night?'

'Not yet. Didn't even have time to find out what Conway looks like. That's why you're here.' He grinned. 'What's your guess about why they're meeting here?'

I gave it some thought. 'Drugs,' I said at last, 'since the flight seems to be out of Miami. Most of the heroin processed in France comes to the United States via South America and Miami, right?'

Randall nodded. 'We figure Conway for a distributor at this end. Sunday night he got a phone call from somebody in South America or Miami, telling him when and where to take delivery of a shipment. That's what he wrote on the flyleaf of your library book. So no wonder he was frantic when his wife gave his list of dates and places to a library cop.'

I suddenly felt tired. I called over to the bartender and ordered a dry martini. I said to Randall, 'So Hatfield's accident could have been murder?'

'Sure. We think it went like this: Mrs. Conway gave you the book, got knocked around by her husband when she told him what she'd done, then on hubby's orders came to you to recover the book for him. When she couldn't do that, or even get the name of the subsequent borrower, her husband did the best he could with the information she *did* get — the borrower's library card number and how you matched it up with his name and address. Conway got the name the same way you did — by phoning what's-her-name at your main desk.'

'Kathy,' I said.

'Yeah. Conway must have gone right

out to Hatfield's when he learned his identity, prepared to do anything necessary to get that book back — or his list on the flyleaf, anyway.' Randall nodded approval of his own theory. 'Conway broke the lock on Hatfield's apartment and was inside looking for the book when Hatfield must have walked in on him.'

'And Conway hid behind the door and clobbered Hatfield when he walked in?'

'Yeah. Probably with a blackjack. And probably, in his panic, hit him too hard. So he faked it to look like an accident. Then he tore the back flyleaf out of your book, thinking nobody would ever notice it was missing.'

'You forgot something,' I said.

'What?'

'He made his wife call me off by telling me he'd found his lost check.'

'I didn't forget it.' Randall grinned.

I said, 'Of course you can't prove any of this.'

'Not yet. But give us time. We get him on a narcotics charge and hold him tighter than hell while we work up the murder case.'

'*If* it's Conway,' I said, looking at my watch, 'who shows up here in twenty-two minutes.'

'He'll show.' Randall was confident. 'Likely get here a little early, even.'

And he did. At 5:56 the original of Mrs. Conway's photograph walked in the door of the Encore Bar. Dapper, young-looking, not much chin under a mustache that drooped around the corners of his mouth. He sat down in the booth nearest the door and ordered a Scotch-and-soda.

Randall threw me a questioning look and I nodded vigorously. Then we talked about baseball until, at 6:14, a bouncy little blonde dish came tripping into the Encore and went straight to Conway's booth, saying loud enough for everybody in the joint to hear, 'Well, hello, darling! I'm so thirsty I could drink *water*!' She looked very pert in her uniform and she had a flight bag over her shoulder. She sat down beside Conway with her back to us.

Randall got up, went to the bar entrance, and opened the door. He stepped out into the vestibule and casually waved one arm over his head, as though he were tossing a cigarette butt away. Then he came back in and leaned against the bar until three young huskies appeared in the doorway. Randall pointed one finger at Conway's booth and the three newcomers stepped over there, boxing in Conway and Miss Harper.

It was all done very quietly and smoothly. No voices raised, no violence. One of the narcotics men took charge of Harper's shoulder bag. The other two took charge of Conway and Harper.

When they'd gone, Randall ordered himself a bourbon and carried it back to our booth and sat down. 'That's it, Hal,' he said with satisfaction. 'Harper had two one-pound boxes of bath powder in her flight bag. Pure heroin. This is going to look very good — very good — on my record.'

I took a sip of my martini and said nothing.

Randall went on, 'You're sure Conway's wife has nothing to do with the smuggling? That she doesn't suspect what her hubby is up to?'

I thought about Mrs. Conway's friendliness, so charming and unstudied. I remembered how the animation and pride I'd seen in her eyes yesterday morning had been replaced by distress and bewilderment in the afternoon. And I said to Lieutenant Randall, 'I'd stake my job on it.'

He nodded. 'We'll have to dig into it, of course. But I'm inclined to think you're right. So somebody ought to tell her why her husband won't be home for dinner tonight, Hal.' He paused for a long moment. 'Any volunteers?'

I looked up from my martini into Randall's unblinking stare. 'Thanks, Lieutenant,' I said. 'I'm on my way.'

2

More than a Mere Storybook

I wasn't ready for his violent reaction. He hurled the heavy glass ashtray at me from point-blank range with the accuracy of a big-league pitcher splitting the strike zone. The tray caught me a stunning blow on the temple and, as they say, I saw stars. Believe, me I did. Plenty of them.

While I sagged on the sofa, dazed and groggy, Campbell scurried into an inner room, came out with an oversize brief-case, and ran for the door like a beagle after a rabbit.

He should have finished me off. By the time he was halfway down the steps to the apartment house lobby, I had gathered my few senses together and was able to stand up and then follow him. My whole life recently seemed to consist of following Herbert Campbell.

I went down the stairway after him two

steps at a time. I caught him before he reached the doorway that led outside. When I put a choke hold on him from behind, none too gently in spite of his being an old man, the fight went completely out of him. He chopped his briefcase as though its handle were red-hot, and began to tear at my forearm across his throat.

I eased up a little as his face congested. 'Pick up your briefcase,' I said, and released him. 'Let's go back upstairs.'

He nodded meekly. He picked up the briefcase and we climbed up the stairway to his apartment. I held his right arm in a businesslike grip. Once back in his living room, he collapsed into an easy chair and began to sob weakly. Keeping a weather eye on him, I lifted his briefcase to the tabletop and opened it up.

It was full of clothing. Shirts, socks, underwear, slacks. Campbell had been about to leave town when I arrived, it seemed. I rummaged around in the case and at the very bottom, under the layers of clothing, I found two books.

I pulled them out and looked at them.

Volume I and Volume II. Their half-calf covers were soiled and stained and worn; a corner of Volume I was bent; there was a slight tear along the spine of Volume II.

Not library books, certainly. One look at the title page of Volume I showed me what they were. I turned another page in Volume I, reverently now, and stared at what was written on the flyleaf in faded brownish-colored ink.

That was when I called Lieutenant Randall of the metropolitan police. I suddenly had the uneasy feeling that Herbert Campbell was too big game for a mere library cop to handle.

* * *

The fourth name on my list for the day was Herbert Campbell at an address on Dennison Avenue. I parked my car a block away and walked to the sleazy apartment house where Campbell lived. The building was a rundown relic of better days.

I went into the vestibule, found out from the mailboxes that Campbell's apartment was number 22, on the second floor, and walked up. I played a tattoo on the door panel of number 22, and after a while the door opened to show me a cherubic, ruddy-faced gent with no chin and a white bristly mustache. He was about 60, I figured, give or take a couple of years, and his head was bald except for an inch of fringe around the edges that matched his white mustache.

Over the raised voices of two women quarreling in a TV soap opera I asked, 'Mr. Campbell?'

'Yes,' he said, giving me a sharp look out of mild blue eyes. 'And who are you?'

'I'm from the public library,' I said politely. 'I've come about all those overdue library books you have, Mr. Campbell.'

'Oh,' he said, and his look of inquiry changed to one of guilt. 'Oh, yes. Come in, won't you? I'm very embarrassed about those books. I know I should've returned them long ago. I got the notices, of course.' He stepped back. I went into his apartment.

It turned out to be surprisingly clean

and attractive. There were a sofa and a round coffee table; two easy chairs, one with a tall bridge lamp beside it and a plastic cushion that showed existence of much sitting, and a floor-to-ceiling wall of bookshelves, well filled, opposite the sofa. The TV was in a corner, going full blast.

He switched off the TV, motioned to a chair, and said, 'Won't you sit down?'

I said, still politely, 'No, thanks. If you'll just give me your overdue library books and the fine you owe, I'll be on my way.'

'Certainly, certainly. I have the books right here.' He gestured at a pile of books on the coffee table. 'I was all ready to bring them back, you see.'

'Why didn't you?' I asked. I began to check the book titles against my list. They were all there.

'I've been sick.' He gave me another treatment of his mild blue eyes.

'Sorry to hear that, Mr. Campbell. You could've renewed the books, you know.'

Campbell was sheepish. 'Well, I must confess, Mr. — ah — '

'Johnson,' I said.

'Yes, I must confess, Mr. Johnson, that there's another reason I'm overdue.' He cleared his throat. 'You see, I quite literally *hate* to return library books. Can you understand that? I have this fierce love for books, any books, and when I have them in my possession it takes all my willpower to make myself let them go. I'd never borrow books at all if I could afford to own enough of my own. Like these.' He waved a thin hand toward his bookshelves. 'I guess I'm what they call a bibliophile. Are you familiar with the term?'

'Sure,' I said. 'I work for the library, remember?'

'Yes. Well then, you can appreciate the minced feelings I have every time I am compelled to return books to the library! I know they don't belong to me, but I am terribly reluctant to give them up. You know? Especially, of course, if I haven't finished reading them.'

'I know,' I said. I'd run into plenty of book nuts. I began to gather his overdue books into a manageable stack. 'You owe us a pretty big fine on this batch, Mr. Campbell.'

'This is the first time I've ever actually *ignored* the overdue notices,' he explained apologetically. 'I did *so* want to finish this one, this novel, before I brought them back.' He tapped the book at the top of the stack, a current bestseller called *Sexless in Salinas*. 'It's so fascinating, so well done, that I can't bear to finish it and end my pleasure. You ever feel that way about a book, Mr. Johnson? Yet I can't bear *not* to finish it, either.' He laughed.

I laughed, too. I'd read that particular book myself. 'Listen, Mr. Campbell, I'll make a deal with you. Pay your fines on all these other books and I'll leave that one with you so you can finish it. Fair enough?'

'Oh, would you? How very kind!' He took *Sexless in Salinas* from the stack, hugged it to his chest, and asked how much he owed me.

I told him. He dipped his hand into his pants pocket and brought out money. While he counted out the fine I idly ran an eye over his bookshelves across the room. Judging from the few titles I could read from that far away, he had the catholic tastes of a true bibliophile. I saw a book on the flora of Nevada, one on weightlifting, and a home-repair guide, cheek by jowl with numerous fiction titles.

Mr. Campbell said, 'There you are, Mr. Johnson. And thanks for being so understanding about my — ah — affliction.' He smiled at me as though at a fellow bibliophile. 'I'll return this one to the library as soon as I finish reading it.'

I nodded and left.

I went back to my car, unlocked it, and added Mr. Campbell's overdue library books to the others I'd already collected. There were a lot of them. Then I crawled under the wheel, started the engine, and headed for the main library downtown. My morning's work was officially over now, except for turning in the overdue books and the fines.

After that I hadn't much to do until lunch except to sit at my desk in the little room behind the business manager's office and indulge my curiosity about that old booklover, Herbert Campbell, who had wanted to finish *Sexless in Salinas* even at the cost of paying another few days' fine.

Well, a phone comes with my office, so I figured it wouldn't cost anything to feed my curiosity. I picked up the telephone and got on to Ellen Corby, one of our librarians who is currently trying to make up her mind whether she'll marry me or not. I asked her if she'd give me the inventory record on *Sexless in Salinas*. She said she would.

She called me back a few minutes later. 'Twenty-seven copies, Hal,' she said. 'It's a popular item.'

'Yeah, no wonder,' I said. 'Have you read it?'

'Of course. Can't you see my maidenly blush?'

'How are the twenty-seven split, Ellen?'

'Six and three,' Ellen said.

'Thanks.' I hung up. You're not supposed to engage in social chitchat on the library's time.

Twenty-seven copies, split six and three. Six at the main library, three at each of our seven branches. My next call was to the checkout desk. 'Inventory says you have six copies of *Sexless in Salinas* circulating,' I said, after identifying myself. 'Can you account for all six?'

'Why?' asked the girl, irritated. 'Are you queer for bestsellers or something?'

'Just answer the question, honey.'

'I'll call you back.'

When she did she said, 'Four are out, one is in the return pile.'

'How about the other one?'

'Gone,' she said. 'No record.'

'Not on the shelf?'

'No. I looked. You want its catalogue number?'

'Never mind. Is one of your 'out' copies on library card XL-392716?' That was Herbert Campbell's library card number on my overdue list.

'Yes,' she said after a minute. 'And incidentally, it's long overdue.'

'Thanks,' I said.

In turn I telephoned all seven of our branches and checked on their copies of *Sexless in Salinas*. Out of the 21 copies supposed to be circulating through the branch libraries, four had vanished without trace.

I sat back in my chair and thought about that for a while. Then I had another idea. I walked down the corridor to the room where our card-catalogue cabinets are. There I went through the cards under the letter 'F' and pretty soon I was looking at a card with the neatly typed book title I was hunting: *The Flora of Nevada.* I took down its number and shelf position and searched the shelves for the book without success. Then I asked Ellen to see if she could locate it for me. She couldn't — neither the book itself nor any record of its having been borrowed. Inventory showed the library had bought only one copy of that book, for the main library. None for the branches. I thought about that, too.

What all this thinking led to, of course, was the conclusion that my friendly bibliophile, Herbert Campbell, was robbing the library blind; and that since I'm a library cop, hired to chase down stolen and overdue books by the public library, I'd better do something about it.

So, after a leisurely lunch at Morris's Cafeteria, I set out again for Dennison Avenue. It was a lovely spring afternoon. Whipped-cream clouds drifted lazily across a delft-blue sky. I caught the delicate fragrance of lilacs through my open car window as I drove. And I wished Ellen Corby would make up her mind to marry me and save me from a lifetime of dreary cafeterias like Morris's.

I parked about a hundred yards south of Campbell's apartment house — the only parking space I could find on the block — got out of my car and started toward the entrance, thinking about what I'd say to him and how tough an act I should put on. Although I'm allowed to carry a gun and make arrests, I didn't figure to need a gun to handle old Campbell, and I hadn't decided yet whether to arrest him or not. That depended on how many of the library's books I could recover and whether he'd be willing to pay the big overdue fines I'd assess on them.

While I was still about fifty yards away, Herbert Campbell came out of the apartment-house entrance carrying a king-size briefcase which seemed pretty heavy, to judge from the way he handled it when he unlocked a gray VW at the curb and maneuvered the briefcase into the back seat. Then Campbell got into the car himself.

I had to make a quick decision — should I brace him now or let it go until later? His briefcase made up my mind. It seemed possible, from its evident weight, that the case contained books. If it did, and the books happened to belong to the public library, I wanted to see where they were going.

So I turned and went back to my car, slid into the driver's seat, and waited until the VW pulled out from the curb. Then I took out after Campbell's car, hanging far enough back so that he wouldn't notice I was trailing him. I hoped.

We played follow-the-leader through light traffic to the South Side. When Campbell pulled up in front of a row of stores on Cameron Way I drove right on by, rounded the next corner, and parked. I ran back to the corner in time to see

Campbell and his briefcase disappearing into the middle shop of the seven in the row.

I debated with myself for half a minute on what to do next, finally lit a cigarette and sat down on a corner bench meant for the convenience of bus riders. From there I could see the entrance to the shop and Campbell's parked car.

In about ten minutes he reappeared on the sidewalk, still carrying his briefcase. Now, though, from the effortless way he swung it into the back of his car, I figured the case was empty. He started up, drove toward me, and went rolling past without even a glance in my direction. Then he took a left at the next block and went out of sight. I let him go.

I walked down the sidewalk to the store Campbell had entered. A sign over the door said: The Red Quill, Edwin Worthington, Prop. The merchandise displayed in the store window was books and more books. My friendly bibliophile, Herbert Campbell, had been paying a visit to the secondhand bookshop. I opened the door and went inside. The interior seemed very dim after the bright sunshine outside, but I could make out tables and racks and shelves of books on every side.

The man standing at the counter at the back of the shop talking on the telephone must be Edwin Worthington, Prop., because he nodded at me when he saw me come in and mouthed silently at me above his telephone receiver, 'Be right with you,' then went back to his conversation.

I browsed idly through his stock of books, paying no attention to him until he said into the phone, 'Octavo, yes, yes, 1719, eh? Good. That's what I thought it was but I wanted to be sure. Thanks very much, Miss Gilchrist. Thanks *very* much!'

He hung up and turned on me one of the most radiant smiles I'd seen recently. His beard tended to hide his mouth, but there was no mistaking the full set of white teeth or the triumphant lilt of his voice when he said, 'Now, then, what can I do for you, sir?' He was feeling very good about something.

'Just browsing, thanks,' I answered him.

He waved a hand. 'Help yourself.'

I stepped over to the fiction shelves and pulled out a copy of *Sexless in Salinas* and thumbed through it. Then, carrying it with me, I drifted over to Worthington, who was leaning against his counter beside the cash register.

I held up *Sexless in Salinas*. 'Isn't this a bestseller?' I asked.

He nodded. 'Second on the list for several months now.'

'Is it available in paperback yet?'

'Not yet.'

'How come you have bestsellers while they're still so popular?'

He shrugged. 'From book club members, estates being settled, people moving away. And of course, from church bazaars, rummage sales, charity book sales of all kinds. Lately I've had a part-time man covering the charity things for me. That book you have there was one of a batch he brought in just a few minutes ago.'

I put the book down on the counter beside his cash register. 'I'll take it,' I said. 'How much?'

'Dollar and a quarter. It's a six ninety-five book.' Then he smiled that big smile again. He was still feeling very expansive. 'I'll let you have it for a dollar today, though.'

'How come?'

'Call it a going-out-of-business price. I'm celebrating. I've had a lucky break and I'm going to close up my shop.'

'Great,' I said. I gave him a dollar. 'Happy retirement, Mr. Worthington.'

Back in my car I examined the secondhand copy of *Sexless in Salinas* with the help of a good magnifying glass I carried on the end of my keychain. I found what I expected: a slight granulation of the inside front cover's end paper where a solvent had been used to remove the card pocket pasted in the front of all library books. The front flyleaf, where the library's name stamp appears, had been cut out. There were barely discernible traces of the library's name stamp lingering on the closed-page edges after treatment with an ink eradicator. And very faint evidence on some of the page margins that the book's identification number had been removed.

What I'd got for my dollar at The Red Quill was one of the library's missing copies of *Sexless in Salinas*, skillfully doctored by a certain bibliophile named Herbert Campbell. So now I not only knew that a thief was robbing the library, but I knew the receiver of his stolen goods. An innocent receiver, I was sure, but a receiver, all the same. So I'd know where to find a lot of our library books after I'd taken care of Campbell.

With that information in my possession, my sense of urgency about Campbell subsided. There was no hurry about arresting him now. I decided to finish my overdue calls that afternoon, take Ellen to dinner and the movies as planned, and get to Campbell first thing in the morning. I felt a little sorry for the old boy, as a matter of fact, even though I knew he was an unmitigated thief.

I was back at the library at quitting time. I walked through the reference department to pick up Ellen for our date and found Annie Gilchrist putting on her jacket to go home. 'Annie,' I said, pausing at her desk, 'you got a telephone call from a Mr. Worthington of The Red Quill bookshop this afternoon about two o'clock, didn't you?'

'Nope,' said Annie, 'I called him. To answer a question he'd phoned in earlier.'

'Whatever you told him on the phone made him so happy,' I said, 'that he gave me a discount on a book I was buying from him at the time.'

'You were *buying* a book?' Annie exclaimed. 'With the whole public library system here to supply you with free reading material?'

'I hate to accept charity,' I said, grinning. 'What was the question you had to look up for Worthington?'

'The date of the first edition of *Robinson Crusoe.*'

'1719?'

'That was it. You must have been eavesdropping.'

'I was. Did Worthington *have* a first edition?'

'He didn't say. Just wanted to be sure of the date.'

'Would a first edition of *Robinson*

Crusoe be worth a lot?'

'Depends on what you mean by a lot. And what condition the first edition is in.'

'Enough for Worthington to retire on?'

She shook her head. 'I doubt it very much, Hal.'

'How much do you think it would be worth?'

'I'll look it up for you tomorrow,' Annie said. 'Right now, if you don't mind, I'm going home.' She grabbed her purse and started out.

'Forget it, Annie,' I called after her. 'I was just curious.'

★ ★ ★

I was knocking at Herbert Campbell's door at nine the next morning. He opened at my second knock and recognized me at once. He was in his shirt sleeves, his fringe of white hair tousled, his eyes as innocent of guile as a child's. Holding the door open a few inches he said, 'Why, hello, Mr. Johnson.'

I said, 'May I come in for a minute?'

'I haven't finished that last book yet.'

'I want to read you something,' I said.

He backed up, puzzled, and I followed him in. 'I don't understand,' he said mildly, 'but whatever it is, read it to me, by all means.' He went to sit in his favorite chair, the one with the dent in the seat cushion.

I read him my Miranda card, informing him of his legal rights. When I finished he stared at me. 'What in heaven's name does *that* mean?'

I sat down at one end of the sofa. 'It means I'm going to arrest you.'

'Arrest me?' His gaze was incredulous. 'What am I supposed to have done?'

'I'll tell you what you've done. You've been stealing books from the public library for months. You've been using your library card to borrow books legitimately at all our branches, and every time you borrowed you walked out with three or four *extra* books under your coat or in your briefcase that you didn't bother to have the librarian check out. You've been bringing these stolen books here to your apartment, removing the library's identification marks, and peddling the books for whatever you can get.'

Campbell shook his head in bewilderment. I plowed on. 'You keep the stolen books here — ' I pointed to his crowded bookshelves. ' — until you think the heat, if any, has died down, using your apartment as a sort of warehouse for stolen books. And you also use it, I might add, to build up your image of a harmless eccentric who loves books so much he just can't bear to part with them. That's why you held those overdue library books until I came to collect them yesterday — so you could impress me with your eccentricity and establish a bibliophile image with the library authorities.'

'Why,' asked Mr. Campbell reasonably, his eyes still mild and puzzled, 'would I try to establish an image like that?' He was toying with a thick glass ashtray on the arm of his easy chair.

'Because you know that in the normal case of book theft from the public library by a bona-fide bibliophile type, all we usually do is hit him with a fine and take back our books. You figured if we ever tumbled to your operation, you would qualify for the same treatment — a fine instead of prison.'

'The only thing wrong with your theory, Mr. Johnson,' said Campbell with dignity, 'is that it happens to be quite untrue. Who, for example, would I sell stolen library books to, for heaven's sake?'

'The Red Quill bookshop, for one,' I answered. 'I talked to Mr. Worthington yesterday.' And that's when he threw the ashtray at me.

★   ★   ★

As it turned out I *was* right to call Lieutenant Randall into the case. He sat across from me in Clancy's Bar and Grill that evening, off duty, and told me about it.

'When we got there,' he said, 'The Red Quill had a penciled sign on the door saying the shop was closed. But there was a light on in the living quarters upstairs — a lamp we could see through the front second-floor window. So we tried to raise Worthington. When we couldn't, we went in and found him at the foot of the flight of steps that leads down from his rooms upstairs. Dead as a mackerel. With a broken neck.'

I murmured, 'Did he fall, or was he pushed?' I was feeling rotten. If I had gone after Campbell yesterday instead of waiting, I might possibly have saved Worthington's life.

'He was pushed,' Randall said.

'How do you know?'

'There was a lump the size of an egg on his head and we found a wrought-iron ashtray upstairs with blood and hair to match.'

I sighed. 'He likes ashtrays.' My temple was still sore.

'Yeah.' Randall's gaze was amused. 'Campbell admits the killing now. Says Worthington told him about the first edition when he delivered those stolen books to The Red Quill yesterday. The first edition was a lucky break — found among hundreds of old books Worthington bought from an estate. The owners never knew what they had, of course.'

'More than a mere storybook,' I murmured.

'What's that?'

'*Robinson Crusoe.* That's how Edward Everett Hale described it.'

'Well,' Randall went on, refusing to be sidetracked by this literary allusion, 'Worthington told Campbell if the *Robinson Crusoe* first edition turned out to be genuine, he was going to close his bookstore and retire. So Campbell went back to The Red Quill about one o'clock last night, killed Worthington, and swiped the book.' Randall grinned. 'Just a harmless, eccentric old book-lover.'

I grunted. 'He's not a real booklover,' I said. 'He wanted to be rich, that's all. Did you notice that signature on the flyleaf of Volume One?'

'Yeah. Some guy's name,' Randall said. 'I can't remember it.'

'Button Gwinnett.'

'Sounds like the head of the sewing circle. Who was Button Gwinnett, for God's sake?'

'Only one of the signers of the Declaration of Independence.'

Randall refused to be impressed. 'Well, well,' he said. 'So he owned a copy of

Robinson Crusoe. So what?'

'A first edition of *Robinson Crusoe*,' I said quietly, 'with Button Gwinnett's signature in it would sell at auction for a quarter of a million dollars, Lieutenant, maybe more.'

'What!'

It was my turn to grin. 'Button Gwinnett signed the Declaration of Independence, all right, but apparently that's about all he *did* sign during his lifetime. Except for Worthington's first edition of *Robinson Crusoe*. Button Gwinnett's signature is one of the rarest — and therefore one of the most valuable — in the whole autograph-collecting field. So you see what a beautiful combination Campbell killed Worthington to get? A first edition of *Robinson Crusoe* autographed by Button Gwinnett. It's fabulous.'

Randall was impressed at last. 'What becomes of the book now?'

'Worthington's heirs get it, I suppose — if he bought it fair and square from that estate.'

'Some legacy,' Randall breathed, 'from

a secondhand bookdealer!' He put his opaque stare on me. 'What tipped you off to this Campbell in the first place?' he asked.

I told him about the song and dance Campbell had given me yesterday about wanting to finish reading *Sexless in Salinas* before I took the book away from him.

'I don't see anything in that,' Randall said.

'You're not a secondhand book expert, that's why,' I explained. 'But *I* am. So I noticed that when Campbell was begging to keep the book so he could finish reading it, he had two *other* copies of *Sexless in Salinas* right there on his bookshelves in plain view.'

3

The Bookmark

Being in the business I'm in — chasing down stolen and overdue books for the public library — I could almost write a book myself on the crazy things people use for bookmarks. Pornographic postcards, hairpins, dog-show ribbons; stalks of celery, marijuana cigarettes. You wouldn't believe the variety. I even found one teenager using the dried skin of a six-inch coral snake. So there was nothing very remarkable about the bookmark I found in Miss Linda Halstrom's overdue library book. At least, I didn't think so at the time.

Miss Halstrom was the third on my list of overdues that day. She lived on the north side in a rundown apartment house that was really an old Victorian mansion converted into a dozen efficiencies. The neighborhood had long since lost its

56

pristine elegance, if it ever had any.

I walked up three flights of rubber-treaded stairs to her apartment and knocked on her door, wiping my forehead with an already sodden handkerchief. The outdoor temperature that July day must have been over ninety. The third-floor landing was dark and dreary-looking and smelled of stale cooking, which made Miss Linda Halstrom, when she answered my knock, seem all the more entrancing to me.

She was dressed in white stretch slacks and a man's shirt with the sleeves rolled up, and looked very cool indeed on such a hot day. Her long, straight blonde hair framed a blue-eyed, high-cheekboned face that now wore an inquiring smile. It was downright refreshing just to look at her.

'Yes?' she asked me brightly in a cool contralto.

'Miss Linda Halstrom?' I countered.

She nodded. I showed her my identification card. 'I'm from the public library,' I said. 'Our records show that you have some library books overdue, Miss Halstrom. I've called to collect the books and the fines you owe.'

A lot of book borrowers get quite indignant at me, for some reason, when I appear at their doors to take back the public library's property. Maybe it's because they feel the library is questioning their integrity by sending me around. Or maybe it's because people tend to resent any kind of police these days — even a library cop like me.

Miss Halstrom, however, was hospitality itself. She apologized profusely for keeping the books so long beyond their due dates. 'Come in, Mr. Johnson,' she invited. 'I have the books right here.'

I followed her into her combination living room-bedroom. The bed, along the far wall, was neatly made up into a day bed, covered with a gaily striped bedspread and strewn with colorful pillows. Everything in the place was as clean and refreshing as Miss Halstrom herself. She pointed to a coffee table by the daybed. 'There they are,' she said, 'three of them. Right?'

'Three is correct.' I picked up the library books and checked them against my list. 'You'll have to pay the fine.'

She shrugged prettily. 'My own fault,' she said. 'I lent them to a friend and forgot all about when they were due. How much is the fine?'

I told her the amount. 'I'll get my purse,' she said, and headed for a closet at the other end of the room while I went through my standard procedure of shaking her three books upside down to see if she'd left anything between the pages.

A small slip of white paper fluttered to the floor from the third book, a suspense story called *The Hub of the Wheel*. The paper landed on the carpet face up, and as I stooped to retrieve it I noted automatically what seemed to be a telephone number written on it in black ink. I picked up the paper and put it on Miss Halstrom's coffee table.

Miss Halstrom found her purse on the closet shelf, crossed the room to me, and counted out the money for her fine. I took it, gathered up her overdue books, and left. I was reluctant to exchange her cool presence for the stifling heat of the streets. But a job's a job.

Going down her stairs, between the second and third floors, I brushed past a short swarthy man in a neat gray suit who was going up. Then I was out in the street again, reaching for my damp handkerchief to resume mopping operations.

I negotiated two blocks of steaming sidewalk between Miss Halstrom's apartment house and my parked car, unlocked the trunk compartment, and fitted her three library books into a big carton. Then I climbed behind the wheel, fired up, and went on about my business.

On my next call I picked up four overdue books from the janitor of a funeral home and came panting back to my car once again, fishing in my pocket for my car keys. I stooped to unlock the trunk and only then realized that this time I wouldn't need a key. Because the trunk was already unlocked. And the lid gaped open about two inches.

Since I'm often careless about locking my trunk, this wouldn't have bothered me at all, except that the trunk lock was twisted out of shape, and the lid showed definite evidence that a prying tool had been used to force it.

Well, the rifling of locked car trunks has become a favorite outdoor sport of the 'disadvantaged' these days, they tell me, so I wasn't too surprised at becoming another victim. I lifted the trunk lid and saw that my carton of books was still there. To the casual eye it looked completely undisturbed.

But my eye is not a casual one; I have an extremely good visual memory. And I distinctly remembered that I had fit Miss Halstrom's three overdue books into my carton with a novel called *Brainstorm* on top. Now the top title was *The Hub of the Wheel* and *Brainstorm* had been demoted to the second place in the stack.

I transferred all the books from the trunk to the back seat of the car, tied the trunk lid down with a piece of cord, and got behind the wheel again, reflecting ruefully that my trunk lock had been destroyed to no purpose. For it was obvious that whoever had broken into my trunk, on finding nothing but a box of library books (used) for his trouble, placidly glanced over some of the titles and then departed in disgust to try for richer spoils elsewhere. A nuisance. But my insurance would take care of the damage to the lock.

At noon I went back to the library and turned in the books and the fines I had collected, ate my lunch in the library cafeteria, and had barely gotten settled at the desk in my tiny office to plan the afternoon's work when my phone rang. Annie, on the library switchboard, said, 'Hal, some girl has been trying to get you for an hour. Where've you been?'

'Eating lunch,' I said. 'Who was she?'

'A Miss Halstrom. I told her you'd call her back when you came in.'

I felt a small thrill of pleasure. 'What are you waiting for then?' I asked Annie.

When Miss Halstrom's contralto came on the line it sounded different. Not so cool and refreshing now. In fact, it sounded on the edge of panic. It said, 'Mr. Johnson?'

'Yes?'

'Are you the man who collected my overdue library books this morning?'

I assured her I was.

'Oh, thank goodness!' she said. 'Will you please do me a favor, Mr. Johnson?'

I said gallantly, 'Just ask me, Miss Halstrom.'

'Well, there was a bookmark in one of my library books, with a telephone number on it, Mr. Johnson. And I have to get it back, please. It's very important. It was in the book called *The Hub of the Wheel*. Do you remember that book?'

'Sure,' I said. 'And it did have a bookmark in it. But I left the bookmark on your coffee table this morning.'

'The coffee table!' Her voice held the beginnings of relief. 'Are you sure? Wait while I look, will you please?' In a moment she was back on the line. 'It's there, Mr. Johnson! Oh, how can I thank you? I'm so *dumb*! I put my purse right down on top of it when I was paying you the money for my fine this morning. No wonder we didn't see it. My boyfriend was furious with me!'

'Boyfriend?' I tried to keep disappointment out of my voice.

In her relief she chattered exuberantly on. 'I *told* you this morning I'd lent the books to a friend. Well, it *was* my boyfriend, and the bookmark with the telephone number on it was *his*, not mine. I didn't even know it was in the book until he came in this morning right after you left and asked for that book because he'd remembered he'd left an important telephone number in it. And I told him you'd just left with the books, so he ran out after you to see if he could reach you and get his bookmark back, but he couldn't find you, so he told me to get that telephone number back for him somehow or I'd be sorry.'

She took a deep breath. 'And now I've got it, and the whole silly thing was just because of my stupidity!' She laughed. 'I'm sorry I bothered you, Mr. Johnson. But I've never seen Jerry so upset!' She hung up.

I remembered the short swarthy fellow I'd passed on her stairway that morning. He must have been Miss Halstrom's boyfriend, and evidently had an ugly temper. And obviously the man was pitifully unworthy of Miss Linda Halstrom, the Scandinavian goddess who had brightened my morning.

It was late the next afternoon before I got around to calling my insurance man to tell him about the broken lock of my car trunk. He said, 'Get it fixed and send the bill to me. You've reported it to the police, of course?'

'No. What's the use? Nothing was taken.'

'Do it anyway,' he told me. 'It has to be on the official record before we can pay any claim on it.'

'I'm police,' I said. 'Don't I count?'

'You're just sissy unofficial fuzz,' he said. 'Report it downtown if you want us to pay the bill.'

So on my way home that evening I stopped off at police headquarters and asked to see Lieutenant Randall. I'd worked for several years in the plain-clothes division under Randall before I took my library job.

Randall was sitting in his office behind a perfectly clear desk, chewing gently on a stogie and regarding the world sleepily through his yellow cat's eyes. He greeted me with a wave of his hand. 'Hi, Hal,' he said blandly. 'You run into some crime at the public library that you can't handle by yourself?'

Just as blandly I answered, 'No, Lieutenant. And if I need help I wouldn't come here for it. I understand the only good detective you ever had in this department resigned five years ago.'

Randall grinned. 'So what do you want?'

'To report a break-in.'

'My, my! Whose?'

'Mine. Somebody jimmied the trunk lid of my car between 10:30 and 10:45 yesterday morning while I was parked in the 9200 block of Cook Street on the north side.'

'Anything stolen?' asked Randall placidly.

'No. But my insurance man won't pay for repairs unless I report the thing officially.'

'Okay,' Randall said. 'You've reported it. You don't expect us to find the culprit, do you?'

'No way.'

'Unless,' said Randall, very bland

again, 'the only good detective we ever had in this department can give us a clue to work on.'

I grinned and started to shake my head. Then I said, 'Wait a minute, Lieutenant. Maybe I *do* have a clue for you.' For echoing in my mind, suddenly and for no reason, was the contralto voice of Miss Linda Halstrom saying to me over the phone: ' . . . so he ran out after you to see if he could catch you and get his bookmark back, but he couldn't find you . . .'

I told Lieutenant Randall about the bookmark business. 'So it's barely possible, isn't it,' I asked him when I'd finished, 'that Miss Halstrom's boyfriend didn't try to catch me at all, but instead followed me in his car until I parked, then jimmied open my trunk, looking for his telephone number? And didn't find it? The only books that showed signs of having been moved in my carton were two of Miss Halstrom's books.'

Randall laughed. 'Some clue! Why would this boyfriend do a thing like that, when he could have just asked you for the bookmark?'

'Maybe he didn't want me to notice the telephone number.'

'Why not?'

'How do I know? But he obviously considered the number important enough to come down hard on poor Miss Halstrom for unknowingly giving it to me.'

'If he couldn't remember the number, why not look it up again, or ask Information for it?'

'Maybe it was an unlisted number.'

Randall blew smoke. 'Do *you* remember it? You used to be good at that.'

I closed my eyes and visualized the slip of paper staring up at me from Miss Halstrom's carpet yesterday. 'Yeah,' I said. I tore a sheet off Randall's desk pad and wrote on it: *Cal 928-4791*.

Randall looked at what I'd written. 'What's the 'Cal'?'

'Layman's shorthand for 'Call,' I guess.'

Randall put his stogie on a battered ashtray, asked for an outside line, and dialed the number. He held his telephone receiver a couple of inches away from his ear so I could hear the distant ringing. After only one ring someone picked up the receiver. A woman's voice said, 'Yes?'

Randall murmured into the phone, 'Is this the Peckinpaugh residence, please?'

'No,' said the voice. 'Wrong number.' And there was a click as she hung up.

'You're losing your charm,' I said to Randall.

Unabashed, he waited a moment, then dialed the number again. The same woman's voice answered immediately. 'Yes?' This time the question was asked in a tight controlled tone, highly charged with either anxiety or anger.

Randall said, 'Who is this, please?'

'Will you kindly stay off this line?' the woman said sharply. 'I'm expecting an important call.' And she hung up again.

'Why didn't you tell her who you are?' I asked Randall.

'I didn't get a chance.' Grimly he dialed the number once more, and when the woman answered he said sternly, 'Now don't hang up, lady, this is the police calling.'

This pronouncement was greeted by an exclamation that was part wail, part sob. 'The police! But we don't *want* the police! Will you please stop tying up this line?' And another click.

Randall's yellow eyes turned thoughtful. ''But we don't *want* the police,'' he murmured. 'An odd turn of phrase, wouldn't you say, Hal?'

'I would. And she sounded quite upset.'

He pushed his phone across the desk to me. 'You try it,' he said. I began to dial. He said, 'Wait.' He was looking at the memo sheet with the telephone number on it. 'What if this 'Cal' doesn't mean 'Call'? What if it's a name? Like short for Calvin, or Calhoun, or something?'

That hadn't occurred to me. I nodded. 'I'll try it.' I dialed the number.

This time, when the receiver was lifted at the other end, I got in first. 'Is Cal there?' I asked brightly.

A sharp intake of breath came clearly over the wire. Then, 'Thank God!' The woman's voice sounded faint and weak. 'Is she all right? You haven't hurt her, have you?' A gulp. Then, with more control, 'I'm doing exactly as you said. I'll have the money ready tomorrow, as soon as the banks open . . . '

Randall was leaning over his desk toward me, listening intently to the small voice at the other end of the wire. I looked into his cat's eyes and raised my eyebrows. He shook his head violently. I said into the telephone, 'Isn't Calvin Brown there? Isn't this 928-3791?' — deliberately giving the wrong number.

Her words stopped as though I'd turned off a faucet. Randall nodded at me and I said hurriedly, 'I'm sorry. I must have dialed it wrong. Excuse it, please,' and hung up.

Lieutenant Randall leaned back slowly in his chair. 'How do you like that?' he said softly.

I said, 'Are you going to barge in on it? She was terrified of police.'

'Not at her end. I want to know who she is, though. And Cal, too.'

An official police demand brought us the information from the telephone company that unlisted number 928-4791 was assigned to a Mrs. Wilson A.

Benedict on Waterside Drive. I whistled. 'She can afford to pay the ransom, I guess. She's the widow of Wilson Benedict, the bank president, isn't she?'

Randall didn't answer. He was already calling the Obituary editor of the *Evening News* who informed us, after he located the clipping in his files, that Wilson A. Benedict, when killed in an auto accident the year before, had been survived by his wife, two college-age sons, and a four-year-old daughter named Callie.

'Callie,' Randall said, picking up his stogie. 'She must be our Cal. Let's go see your Miss Halstrom.'

I was already on my feet. 'Right,' I said, just as though I still worked for him.

Five minutes after we found her partaking of a late dinner in her apartment on the north side, Randall had extracted the following information from a distressed but cooperative Miss Halstrom. Item: her boyfriend's name was Jerry Gates. Item: he was chauffeur-handyman for a wealthy family named Carson on Waterside Drive and lived in their garage apartment. Item: the Carsons were on vacation in the mountains. Item: Jerry Gates was going to marry Linda Halstrom as soon as he got the large legacy he was expecting from an uncle who had died while Jerry was serving as a medic in Vietnam several years ago, before Jerry had even met Linda. And item: the telephone number on his missing bookmark, according to Jerry, was that of the lawyer, name unknown, whom he was supposed to call to find out when he could expect his legacy.

Well, that was enough information for Randall. We left Halstrom weeping into her cold TV dinner and took off for Waterside Drive. En route, Randall called headquarters and ordered reinforcements to meet us. He wanted to leave me out of it, but he couldn't waste time arguing, so I went along. When the reinforcements arrived, there were six of us, counting me — a small army.

As it turned out we didn't need that many, but we didn't know that till later. It was full dark by the time we reached Waterside Drive. A promise of coming coolness was faintly detectable in the overheated July air. We drove past the stone entrance pillars twice before we left the cars a block away and drifted back, in shifts of two, trying to look inconspicuous as we ducked inside and melted into the gloom of the trees that lined the drive.

When we were all there, gathered in the dense shadow of a huge sycamore, Randall looked over the setup. The enormous turn-of-the-century house, covered with gingerbread scrollwork that was faintly visible to us in the starlight, squatted at the end of the driveway like an obscene insect. Not a single light shone in it. Off to the right, maybe 30 yards from the house and placed out of sight from the street, was an old-fashioned two-car garage, originally a carriage house in all probability, with the chauffeur's quarters above it. We could see a light shining from the front windows of the garage apartment.

Randall pointed to the light. 'That's it,' he whispered. He looked up at the gnarled limbs of the sycamore that sheltered us and said, 'O'Neill, get up in this tree with your field glasses and see

74

what you can see.'

We waited then in complete silence, broken only by the scrape of shoe leather on rough tree bark, while O'Neill climbed the tree. Every few feet he'd stop and take a look through the field glasses to see if he was high enough to get a view into the lighted windows of the chauffeur's quarters. Finally he settled on a thick branch about 25 feet up and trained his glasses on the windows for several minutes without moving.

'Well?' asked Randall as O'Neill came sliding down the tree.

'One guy,' said O'Neill, barely loud enough to be audible. 'Sitting in an easy chair reading the newspaper. *The Evening News.*'

'Could you see the whole room? Only one guy? You're sure?'

O'Neill nodded. 'I'm sure.'

Randall shook his head. 'One doesn't seem enough.'

'Maybe there are guards outside,' I suggested.

'You keep out of this,' Randall told me. Then, to two of the others, 'Jim, make a

75

circuit of the house. And you, Lew, take the garage. No noise, you hear? Just see if you can locate any guards around. And if you do, fade out. Come back here. Don't take any aggressive action of your own. Understood?'

Jim and Lew slid away without a word. We waited again. I needed a cigarette. But then, so did the others, probably. Twenty minutes crept by. O'Neill was up in the tree again, keeping in view the man reading the newspaper in the garage apartment.

'No guards that we could see,' Jim reported when he and Lew rejoined us.

'Huh!' said Randall. He seemed disappointed. 'Only one guy. Any other lights visible?'

'None in the main house,' Jim said.

'And only in the garage in that front room upstairs,' Lew said. 'The back windows are dark. Or back window, rather. There's only one.'

Up in the tree O'Neill spoke. 'The guy's getting up from his chair. Going to a door at the back end of the room. Opening it. Going through. It's a little hallway. He's gone now.'

Randall nodded. 'Come on down, O'Neill.' He turned to Lew. 'Any place behind the garage where we can look through that rear window with the glasses?'

'Yeah,' Lew answered. 'A tree bigger than this one. Except there's no light.'

'Come on,' Randall muttered, and we followed him as silently as we could toward the garage, clinging to the shadows. At the foot of the outside staircase that led up to the garage apartment Randall said, 'Lew and Jim, stay here in the angle of the wall until I tell you different. O'Neill, take the garage doors — there might be an inside exit. Shenkin, under the back window. Nail anybody who tries to get out of that upstairs apartment. Got it? And Hal,' he said, 'you come with me.'

I nodded. Randall took the field glasses from O'Neill and led me quickly around to the back of the garage, Shenkin trailing us and taking position under the back window as instructed.

'I want to see what's in that back

room,' Randall said to me. He gestured toward the big tree Lew had reported. 'Climb up there and give it a try, will you?'

'I'm no tree climber. I thought you wanted me out of it?'

'I do. That's why I'm sending you up the tree.' His yellow eyes glittered in the starlight. 'Get going.' He tilted his head to look up at the rear window. 'Maybe reflected light from the front room will show you something.'

'And if I see anything?'

'If you see enough to show you we're right about this screwy deal, whistle. We'll take it from there.'

I climbed up the tree as silently as I could manage it. I sat with the glasses trained on the small rear window of the garage apartment for ten long minutes before I could report anything to Randall below. Then a door opened and a path of light cut into the darkness of the back room I was watching. The shaft of light began at the opening door and ended at a bed on the left side of the room. A girl lay on the bed, sleeping.

I whistled softly. Immediately I could hear Randall taking off and running hard for the front of the garage. In another moment the sound of rushing feet on wooden steps thundered in the night, and Randall's voice, perfectly clear to me up in my tree, shouted, 'Open up! This is the police!'

I kept my glasses trained on the man who had entered the back room. Randall's shout caught him just as he bent over the sleeping girl. He straightened galvanically. He cast one incredulous look toward the front of the garage, then turned and came charging directly toward me.

With hands and arms stiffened before him to protect his head, he hit the rear window of the room in a long horizontal dive that carried away window glass, sash, and sticks of frame. It was like watching a TV detective leap through a breakaway window. In the midst of the window explosion the man tumbled out into the night air 15 feet above the unprepared head of Shenkin, dutifully parked under that back window.

I yelled, 'Shenkin! Watch out below!' But it was too late. Shenkin looked up, jerked right, then left, trying to avoid the falling object. He failed. The man's hurtling body landed feet first on Shenkin's head and shoulders and drove him to the ground as effectively as a pile driver.

Transfixed for a few seconds in my tree, I waited for Shenkin to move. He didn't. He was out cold. And the man who had leaped from the window — Jerry Gates, presumably — was in little better condition. He seemed badly shaken by his fall. It took him roughly forty seconds to stagger to his feet, look around muzzily and set off again, straight toward my tree.

By that time I was heedlessly removing square inches of hide from my arms and ankles, shinnying down my tree backward as fast as I could slide without going into freefall. The field glasses hung from my neck on their strap and set up a clatter as they bumped against the tree trunk during my hasty descent.

A reverberating crash from the front of

the garage informed me that Randall and Jim and Lew had broken down the front door of the apartment. I was aware of this only on the fringe of my attention, which was centered strongly now on Jerry Gates. He was running toward me unsteadily as I reached the foot of my tree.

I was in deep shadow there. He didn't see me. So I did the only thing I could think of to stop him. I swung Randall's heavy field glasses on the end of their carrying strap once around my head for momentum, like a cowboy twirling a rope, and let them fly.

They caught the fugitive just above the right temple, making a thump of their own to add to the assorted violent sounds of that night. And he went down for the count even more gracefully than poor unlucky Shenkin.

When Randall burst through into the garage apartment's back room a moment later, with his gun out, he found that little Callie Benedict had slept peacefully through all the fireworks.

★   ★   ★

The next day the police were heroes in the newspapers and on TV. For when little Callie was returned, unharmed and without payment of the ransom, Mrs. Benedict couldn't say enough nice things about 'those marvelous policemen'. I was mentioned in the news reports as a former cop who had inadvertently alerted the police to the kidnapping during a routine report of a car break-in. They didn't even mention my name.

Lieutenant Randall called me at the library at noon. 'We got the story out of Gates,' he said. 'I'll fill you in. The only solo kidnapping attempt in my experience. Living next door to the kidnap victim made it almost work for him.'

'How'd Gates grab the girl?' I asked.

'She's got a pet rabbit in a hutch by the hedge that forms the boundary line between the Benedicts and the Carsons. Every afternoon at five o'clock the kid goes out to feed her rabbit. So Gates just reached through the hedge from his side, slapped a chloroform pad over the kid's face, and carried her up to his garage apartment. Then he gave her a shot of drugs to keep her out of it until he collected the ransom from her mother. He swears he was going to turn her loose — unharmed, of course. And he was counting on Mrs. Benedict's promise not to call us in. Any questions?'

'Where'd he get the unlisted phone number?'

'Three weeks ago in a bar after a few drinks with a guy who used to be the Benedicts' chauffeur.'

'And 'Cal' was a code word to identify the kidnaper to Mrs. Benedict?'

'Yeah.'

'Okay,' I said. 'No more questions. But I've got a big fat complaint.'

'Let me guess. Your feelings are hurt because we didn't give you a fair share of glory in the public prints, right?'

'It would've been great publicity for the library.'

'And for you, too, hey?'

'You could've given them my name, at least. It wouldn't've hurt you any.'

Randall chuckled. 'It wouldn't've hurt me, no. But it would've hurt the department, Hal.'

'For God's sake! How?'

'Well — ' Lieutenant Randall was at his blandest. ' — don't you think it might destroy public confidence in the police department if I let it be publicly known that the only real *good* detective we ever had in the department resigned five years ago?'

4

The Elusive Mrs. Stout

It was ten minutes before nine o'clock on a cool September morning when I guided my old Chevy into the parking lot of The Scottish Arms.

The Scottish Arms is a twenty-story residential tower of stainless steel and marble, a very exclusive address. It stands in lonely grandeur on the eastern outskirts of the city where there's plenty of room for ground-level parking and no urgent necessity for rich (and usually elderly) tenants to tool in and out of a smelly subterranean garage every time they want to take a drive.

I left the Chevy angled into the curb at a spot marked GUEST, and headed for the main entrance to the apartment house, thinking with amusement how forlorn my battered car looked in the midst of the shiny Cadillacs, Continentals and Imperials belonging to the tenants of The Scottish Arms.

I was glad, though, that my first call that day was at The Scottish Arms. For although I'm only a library cop who specializes, if you can call it that, in recovering stolen and overdue books for the public library, I like to start my day out with a little class as much as anyone.

The main lobby of The Scottish Arms was classy, all right, if you think fake neo-Gothic verticality is classy. Everything was tall and narrow, from the entrance doors and tinted windows to the long thin crystal tubes that made up the chandelier hanging from the ceiling.

Mrs. J. W. Stout, in apartment 18B, was the object of my researches this morning among the well-to-do. Where most women who dwelt in The Scottish Arms, if they read books at all, probably bought them by the carton from their book clubs or booksellers, my Mrs. J. W. Stout was apparently a girl who borrowed books by the bagful from the public library — and forgot to bring them back. According to my list she had 12 books — all new fiction titles — that were now five and one-half weeks overdue and had accumulated fines to the grand total of $18.90 — a magnificent fine, even for a resident of The Scottish Arms.

There are a lot of reasons why people who borrow books from the public library fail to return them on time. Mrs. J. W. Stout's reason, I was quite sure, was merely forgetfulness: in the flurry and confusion of other interests, Mrs. Stout simply forgot about her library books. That she must *have* outside interests seemed evident, because she was never at home. I'd come to apartment 18B on three separate occasions in the past two weeks to collect her books and fines and I had yet to find her at home. But this morning she had answered my phone call, and promised to wait for me.

I crossed the lobby to the elevators, entered an empty car, and pushed the button for the eighteenth floor. When the car whispered to a stop and the doors slid soundlessly open, I stepped out into a circular landing, deeply carpeted. Not counting the elevator doors, there were only three doors opening onto this small lobby. One was the door to the fire stairs. One had the gilded inscription 18A on it, just under the round peephole. And the third door was mine — rather, Mrs. Stout's — 18B.

I walked over to it and pressed the button. I could hear chimes faintly through the door, sending musical notes throughout Mrs. Stout's apartment to announce my arrival.

Nothing happened.

I waited patiently for a minute. Then I thumbed the button again and waited some more. Still nothing. At first I was surprised, next puzzled, and finally, as no response came to my ringing, irritated.

I leaned close to the door and listened for sounds of movement behind it. I heard nothing. Applying one eye to the peephole, I tried to look inside, but without success. The peephole gave only one-way vision. People inside could see out, but people outside could not see in. All that the people outside could see was a distorted reflection of themselves in the peephole.

Irritation won out over surprise and puzzlement. I turned away from 18B and tramped through the thick rug to the door of 18A and gave *that* button a good solid treatment. I suppose my rising temper must have been reflected in the violence with which I pressed the button, because it wasn't more than thirty seconds until the door opened with a snap and I was facing a middle-aged woman with dyed blonde hair and no eyebrows at all. She was apparently just getting up, because she had on a silk dressing gown of indeterminate color, somewhere between violet and purple, flowered bedroom slippers on her small feet, and held a half-eaten piece of toast in one hand.

The skin where her eyebrows should have been rose questioningly when she saw me. 'Yes?' she asked in a no-nonsense voice, and then, before I could reply, she added fretfully, 'I'm not *up* yet, for heaven's sake! It's so *early*! Who are you?'

'Hal Johnson,' I said. 'From the public library.' I showed her my identification card. 'I called to collect some overdue books from your neighbor, Mrs. Stout, but she doesn't seem to be at home.'

'She's never home,' said 18A. 'Vera's busy, busy, busy. So what do you want from me? I haven't any overdue books. And I'm right in the middle of my breakfast.'

'I'm sorry to disturb you,' I said. 'I thought perhaps you would know if Mrs. Stout has gone out. I telephoned her early this morning that I was coming for her books and she said she'd stick around until I got here.'

18A laughed. 'Vera's got a memory like a sieve,' she said. 'She probably forgot you the minute she put down the phone.'

'Probably,' I said, sighing. 'You didn't see or hear her leave, did you?'

'Of course not! Do you think I spy on my neighbors? Especially a dear friend like Vera?' She put the rest of her toast into her mouth and chewed daintily. 'Her husband left for work a while ago, that's all I know. But Vera wasn't with him. He was talking to some other man in the elevator. I could hear him.' She swallowed. 'That was when I opened my door to get my morning newspaper.'

'Well, thanks,' I said. 'I guess I'll just have to try her again.'

'Do that; only next time you can save yourself the trip all the way up here to the eighteenth floor by checking first to see if Vera's car is in the parking lot. If it's not there, you'll know Vera isn't here, either.'

'I'll remember that,' I said. 'What kind of car does she drive?'

'Green Pontiac,' she said, closing the door. She would be quite an attractive woman, I thought, once she penciled in her eyebrows for the day. I hoped her breakfast coffee was still hot.

I rang for the elevator, dropped to the lobby, and walked out to the parking lot, still more than a little miffed at Mrs. Stout for standing me up. If you're rich, you can afford to be forgetful, I suppose.

I got into my Chevy and was backing out to leave when I noticed that the two parking slots next to mine were marked 18B. One for Mr. Stout, no doubt, and the other for Mrs. Stout. Mr. Stout's slot was empty. In the other one stood a green Pontiac.

I hesitated, then pulled back into my GUEST slot, telling myself I was damned if a scatterbrained, forgetful woman was going to get the better of me in a matter involving 12 library books and a fat fine of $18.90. Mrs. Stout had probably been standing behind her door the whole time I was ringing her chimes, watching me through her peephole!

I marched myself back into the main lobby of The Scottish Arms and went over to the elevator. The indicator dial showed a car on its way up. The light for the 18th floor came on and stayed red for a few seconds; the elevator had obviously stopped there. All at once I felt certain it had been summoned to bring my elusive Mrs. Stout down to one of her outside activities, now that the bothersome man from the library had been gotten rid of.

I grinned at the thought. I would stop her as she stepped out of the elevator. If necessary, I'd make a real nuisance of myself. Unless it was the eyebrow-less lady from 18A who was descending? Hardly likely; I thought; she must still be without her eyebrows and in her dressing gown. However, I'd better be sure before I acted. I stepped to one side of the elevator door and took cover behind a large artificial plant in a massive blue pot.

It wasn't a woman, however, who stepped from the elevator. It was a man. A man who, from his back view as he crossed the lobby, seemed to be on the youngish side, with medium-long black hair curling over the collar of his plaid sports coat. He moved jauntily, as though very pleased about something.

I need hardly say that he took the wind right out of my sails. For now it appeared there might be more to Mrs. J. W. Stout than met the eye. Was she not only an embezzler of books from the public library, but also an immoral wife who clandestinely entertained young men in her private apartment only minutes after her husband, poor hard-working fellow, had left for the office? If so, no wonder she had refused to answer her door.

Yet why did she tell me to come for my books this morning if she expected *her* young man's visit to coincide with mine?

Simple. She hadn't expected her boy-friend, if that's what he was, to arrive when he did. But, I asked myself severely, what if the guy was the husband of the lady in 18A? Or her boyfriend? Or somebody who just happened to emerge from the fire stairs on the 18th floor and take the elevator the rest of the way down? Or even, perhaps, a door-to-door salesman, canvassing The Scottish Arms in defiance of the sign in the main lobby forbidding it?

All the while I was mulling this over, I was skulking out to the parking lot behind the young man in question, keeping far enough behind him to interpose several Cadillacs and Continentals between his back and my eyes.

He went straight to Mrs. Stout's green Pontiac.

He climbed behind the wheel and started the engine.

That eliminates the lady in 18A, I told myself, watching him turn into Spartan Drive and head west in the Pontiac. *And that eliminates the fire stairs stranger, too*, I thought, *and the door-to-door salesman. So what am I left with? Either Mrs. Stout's boyfriend, or —* I fired up my Chevy and backed around — *a guest of Mrs. Stout's who, for some reason unknown, refused to allow her to answer my ring at her doorbell. Or someone who, in Mrs. Stout's absence, refused to answer her doorbell himself. But why?*

I turned the Chevy west on Spartan Drive and almost cheerfully began to follow Mrs. Stout's green Pontiac through the early-morning traffic. I kept asking myself why I was neglecting my own job to pry into the private affairs of Mrs. J. W. Stout, whom I had never even met but who owed the public library the astonishing fine of $18.90. I had no good answer to this question, yet my foot kept bearing down on the accelerator and my eyes stayed doggedly fixed on Mrs. Stout's car, now being driven toward an unknown destination by an unknown young man.

Still, I reflected, I was my own boss. Why shouldn't I indulge my natural curiosity if I wanted to? And I wanted to. I had a definite feeling about the young man in Mrs. Stout's Pontiac.

We went at moderate speed through Elmersville and Conshocklie, heading over west. I stayed on the Pontiac's trail, but far enough back to avoid, I hoped, the attention of the young man driving it. Once we hit the four-lane interstate from Conshocklie west, I could make an accurate guess as to where we were going.

The Tricounty Airport. There wasn't anything else out this way except 75 uninspiring miles of farmland between the airport and Culmertown. Ten minutes later the Pontiac turned into the airport. I turned in after it and followed it, not too closely, until it entered the huge east parking lot, whereupon I turned the other way, into the west lot. I took my ticket from the gatekeeper, parked the Chevy in the first vacant place I came to, and made for the terminal building.

Mrs. Stout's young man was there before me. When I came into the domed rotunda, I saw him standing in the queue of passengers before the Eastern Airlines counter. He had an Eastern ticket in his hand but no luggage of any kind.

I went to the newsstand that flanks

Eastern's counter on the left and pretended to be looking through a copy of a magazine. From the corner of my eye I saw my quarry gain the counter and hand his ticket to the clerk. I came to the front of the newsstand in time to hear the clerk's words as he gave the ticket back to Mrs. Stout's young man after checking it. 'Flight 837,' he said. 'Departure Gate 6.'

I turned my back quickly and bent my head over my magazine as he idled momentarily in the open corridor and then headed for the airport lunchroom, designated by a sign over its entrance as The Coronado Restaurant.

Casually I trailed after him, pausing at Eastern's counter only long enough to note from the posted departure schedule that Flight 837 for St. Louis departed at 10:45.

The wide glass partition that separated The Coronado Restaurant from the terminal rotunda gave me an unobstructed view of the interior. Mrs. Stout's young man was settling himself on a high stool among a dozen or so other customers at the quick-service counter.

He was tapping his fingers in a relaxed way on the countertop as he waited for a menu. The wall clock in the restaurant showed the time to be 10:03.

I began to feel pretty silly, spying on a citizen who was probably quite innocent of any wrongdoing. He *had* to be either Mrs. Stout's lover, I told myself, or a friend or a relative. He'd had her car keys, hadn't he? And there had been nothing furtive or surreptitious about his actions. Casual, untroubled, and jaunty — that was Mrs. Stout's young man. I still had a feeling about him, though. Maybe it was his jaunty air.

He put sugar and cream into the coffee the waitress brought him and stirred it languidly with a spoon. While he did so, his eyes sought the lunchroom entrance doors several times.

That decided me. I went over to the rank of pay phones along the far wall of the rotunda, closed myself into one of the booths, dropped my dime, dialed police headquarters, and asked for Lieutenant Randall. I'd worked under him for several years in the detective division of the city police.

When I got through to him he said, 'Lieutenant Randall,' in a noncommittal voice.

'Hal Johnson,' I said. 'I've got a problem you might be able to help me with, Lieutenant.'

'Really, Hal? *You* need help? A smart ex-cop like you?' His tone was dulcet but dripped with sarcasm.

'A police problem, Lieutenant,' I said. 'At least it *could* be. You can help me find out.'

His manner changed at once. 'What is it, Hal?'

I told him about my abortive call on Mrs. Stout and about the young man who had driven off in her car so blithely, and that I now knew where said young man could be reached if it developed he had done anything to break the law.

'Where are you now?' Randall went right to the heart of it.

'The airport. I can see our young man from this pay phone.'

'Oh?' He waited for more.

'Yeah. He's having coffee in the

lunchroom. His flight for St. Louis leaves in exactly forty minutes.'

'What do you suggest?'

'Send a radio car to The Scottish Arms. Check on Mrs. Stout's apartment. Get a look inside it on some excuse or other. Suspected auto theft, maybe. Or an anonymous tip that her place has been burglarized. Then call me back here and let me know the score.'

'I guess I can do that.'

'Thanks.' I gave him the number of the pay phone I was using. 'I'll wait right here until I hear from you.'

'Give me fifteen minutes.'

I half-opened the door of the telephone booth, leaned against it, and waited as patiently as I could to find out whether I was a suspicious fool or a very perceptive library cop. Mrs. Stout's young man went right on drinking his coffee, unperturbed. His head, though, it seemed to me, turned more frequently toward the lunchroom doors with the slow passage of time. I took what comfort I could from that while I waited.

I smoked two cigarettes down to

nubbins before the telephone at my elbow jangled. I glanced at my wristwatch as I closed the door and took down the receiver. I had to hand it to Randall. Seventeen and one-half minutes.

I said into the phone, 'Well?'

'Car 67 just reported finding your Mrs. Stout tied into a chair and gagged with a napkin in apartment 18B of The Scottish Arms.'

I blew out my breath. 'What does she say happened?'

'Nothing.'

'Nothing?'

'She's in shock. Fainted. Went out like a light when they untied her. That guy of yours still there?'

'Finishing his coffee.'

'Grab him,' Randall said. 'I've got two men on the way.'

'Grab him — ? Listen, Lieutenant, he's twice as big as I am and half as old. I need help.'

'You're getting it.'

'What if your men can't make it here before Flight 837 leaves?'

He hesitated. Then, 'Stay where you

are. I'll call the airport police to lend you a hand. Okay?'

'Okay.' I hung up.

I figured it ought to take the Lieutenant about two minutes to alert the airport police. That would still give us plenty of time to detain Mrs. Stout's young man before plane time. I began to relax a little as I waited for the airport cops to show.

Somebody else showed first. A tall heavy-set man in his thirties left the Eastern checkout counter and went like a homing pigeon to the lunchroom stool to the right of the one occupied by the guy who stole Mrs. Stout's Pontiac. He wore a conservative business suit, polished black shoes, a narrow establishment-type necktie. He carried an oversize briefcase in one hand.

As he settled himself on his stool, he said a few words to his neighbor. Then they both glanced up at the wall clock and the newcomer said something to the waitress behind the counter. After that, conversation languished. My nerves tightened up again. Now there seemed to be two malefactors for me to handle — and the new one was even bigger and more formidable than the first one.

Oh well, I thought, counting the airport police and me, and Randall's troops, there would be at least five of us to their two. The trouble was, I was still all by myself on the battle line and the time for Flight 837's departure was drawing closer. I lit another cigarette. It tasted awful.

Presently two husky men with airport police patches on their shirt sleeves drifted up to my telephone booth and raised their eyebrows at me. I nodded, stepped out of the booth, and drew them across the rotunda until we were out of sight of the lunchroom counter. Then I said, 'Listen, there are two men in the lunchroom — '

'Two?' said one of the cops in surprise. 'City police said one.'

'He's been joined by a pal,' I said, 'and the lunchroom's half full of people, so you can't operate in there. Too many bystanders might get hurt.'

'Then where?' asked the second cop.

'How about the gate before they board

103

their plane? Flight 837. Eastern. Gate 6. I don't want them to see your sleeve patches, though. They might smell a rat.'

'We'll put on jackets. How do we recognize them?'

I said, 'I'll go into the restaurant and keep an eye on them until their flight is called, and an eye out for the city cops who are on their way. When the two approach the barrier to be processed by the skyjacking machine, I'll be right behind them, maybe with the city cops, too. I'll tip you the sign. The main thing is, I don't want anybody hurt.'

'Neither do we.' And they drifted off.

I swallowed a dry lump in my throat and walked into the lunchroom. Threading my way between tables, I came to rest on the stool at the counter at the left of Mrs. Stout's young man. The clock on the wall said it was now 10:28. Seventeen minutes until flight time. I ordered coffee from the waitress when she came along. It was black and strong, and when I took a gulp of it I burned my tongue. I wondered idly whether Lieutenant Randall's men would get there in time for zero hour.

At 10:32 the man beside me turned his head my way and spoke in a soft, slow drawl. 'Look under the counter,' he murmured.

I was startled. 'Under the counter?'

'Yeah.'

I looked under the counter. His hand, lying in his lap and partially concealed by his yellow lunchroom napkin, held a short-barreled gun pointed at my right kidney.

'What's that for?' I said, forcing myself to take another sip of coffee.

'For curious old jerks who don't mind their own business.' He smiled at me.

His friend with the narrow necktie was looking at him sideways. 'What's all this?' he said in a bored voice.

'This guy was snooping at Stout's apartment an hour ago,' the younger man explained. 'Ringing the doorbell. Trying to get in.' He turned a cold, colorless stare on me and moved the gun in his lap. 'You followed me here from The Scottish Arms. Why? You a cop?'

'A cop?' I tried to laugh but it came out

hollow and shaky. I was thinking what a brainless dummy I'd been to come boldly into the lunchroom, drawing attention to myself. For this guy had obviously viewed my rugged features before — through the peephole in Mrs. Stout's apartment door. So naturally he recognized me the minute I sat down beside him in the lunchroom.

His friend didn't seem unduly worried. He calmly drained the last of his coffee and glanced once more at the wall clock. 'I think he has to go to the men's room,' he said with the suggestion of a smile.

Mrs. Stout's young man nodded. 'Good a place as any.' He motioned to the waitress for their checks. Then he asked her for mine, too. I kept quiet. If you've ever had a gun barrel only four inches from your kidney, you'll understand why.

The man with the narrow tie took the checks, reached under his stool for his briefcase, and headed for the cashier's desk. Under his breath he said, 'Meet you on the plane, Joe.' His manner was composed.

Joe slipped his gun into his side jacket pocket but kept his hand on it. 'Men's room,' he said to me. 'No tricks.'

Meekly I preceded him out of the lunchroom into the rotunda, down the transverse corridor toward a sign that said 'Men' in brass nailheads. Joe was only a step behind me, practically breathing down my neck. The loudspeakers began to call Flight 837. The man with the briefcase wandered off toward Gate 6.

I didn't know what Joe had in mind for me in the men's room, but I knew it wouldn't be pleasant. In fact, it might even be fatal if the room should happen, by ill chance, to be empty when we got there.

My luck was running sour. The men's room was as empty as a sleepwalker's eyes.

'Well, well,' said Joe's soft drawl over my shoulder. 'Go into the stall at the far end, baby.' I risked looking back at him for an instant. All I saw was his hand coming out of his jacket pocket, still holding the gun, only now he was holding it by the barrel. I breathed a sigh of relief. It seemed I was going to get conked with a gun butt. That's bad enough. But it's much better than getting shot in the kidney.

I stepped briskly, therefore, to the end stall. I was almost there when I heard a soft thud behind me. I risked another glance behind. And this time I saw a beautiful sight.

Joe was still behind me, but he had come to a sudden stop. Both hands, including the one holding his gun like a club, were raised above his head. Over his shoulder grinned the homely Irish face of Detective Second Class Herb O'Neill, and close behind him loomed Detective Third Class Terry Shenkin, who was reaching up a hand to relieve Joe of his short-barreled gun. The reason for the tableau was that O'Neill had his own police positive shoved into the small of Joe's back so hard I expected to see its snout emerge from his belt buckle. The soft thud I'd heard was the men's room door closing.

I turned around. O'Neill said, 'Is this the monkey Lieutenant Randall wants, Hal?'

'Yeah,' I said weakly.

'Good. Cuff him and we'll take him out to the car,' O'Neill said to Shenkin.

I looked at my watch. 'We can pick up another monkey to go with him if we hurry,' I said. 'At Gate 6. We've got four minutes.'

Shenkin put the cuffs on Joe, who hadn't said a word, not even a four-letter one, since my friends had arrived. O'Neill and I ran out of the men's room and put on speed for Gate 6.

'Where'd you drop from?' I panted as we hurried along.

'Came into the terminal and saw you coming out of the lunchroom with that monkey walking too close behind you in what we call a threatening posture,' O'Neill said. 'No magic about it, Hal.'

'For me it *was* magic,' I said. 'Thanks, Herb. Now slow down.'

We approached Gate 6. I spotted the two airport cops idling in the crowd around the boarding gate. Joe's pal with the narrow tie was standing fifth in the line of passengers, waiting his turn for the skyjacking frisk. Every few seconds he turned his head to check on whether Joe was going to make the plane.

I ducked my head and brushed imaginary dust off my trousers just in time. He didn't see me. As soon as his back was toward us again, I snaked through the crowd, O'Neill trailing, to one of the airport cops and said to him, 'This is O'Neill, city police. And the fifth man in the boarding line is the one we want.'

'You said there was two,' he said, giving me a funny look. I didn't blame him.

'We nailed him upstairs. Can you take this one? The guy with the narrow necktie?'

'We can take him. Come on, Al,' he said to his partner. They had put dark jackets on over their police shirts.

'I'll be right behind you if you need me,' O'Neill said. It was their turf.

They didn't need him. Or me, either. They closed in from behind on the big man and took him out of the crowd at the boarding gate like the professionals they were. One on each arm, holding him up as though he'd grown suddenly faint, murmuring soothing remarks to the people nearby about getting him to the sick bay. It was slickly done.

The guy was too surprised to do much more than struggle weakly as they led him out of the crowd. By the time they bundled him over to O'Neill and me, waiting behind a soft-drink machine, everybody had turned back to the boarding gate and forgotten all about him.

'Thanks a million, boys,' I said to the airport cops. Then to O'Neill, 'You want to take the prisoner? I'll take the briefcase.'

I got the best of that bargain. For the briefcase contained $92,000 in hundreds, fifties, twenties, and tens. The paper bands around the bundles of bills said 'First Fidelity Savings and Loan'.

'Yeah,' Lieutenant Randall told me five minutes later when I telephoned him from a pay phone to report the money, 'your Mrs. Stout's husband is the big boss at First Fidelity. We just got a call ten minutes ago that his secretary found him locked in his private can at the office, out cold, gagged and tied up. And the cashier says there's ninety-two thousand missing from the vault. Looks like you found it, Hal.'

'Lucky me,' I said. 'So that's how they worked it, hey? Forced their way into Stout's apartment, and Joe held Mrs. Stout hostage while his buddy went with Mr. Stout to his office and made him cooperate in getting the dough from the vault or Joe would do something violent to Mrs. Stout.'

'And arranged to meet at the airport and leave town,' Randall said. 'The Stouts will tell us about it when they're fit to talk. Both are in the hospital — shock and mild concussion.'

'Too bad,' I said. 'I hope there's a reward, Lieutenant. I could use some extra dough.'

'No reward. The insurance company doesn't even know First Fidelity was robbed and we've already recovered the loot. So why a reward?'

'Something to show for my wasted morning,' I said.

Randall laughed. 'Don't pester me with your little problems. I got enough of my own. Send in the ninety-two grand with O'Neill and the hoods, will you?'

'No,' I said.

'No?'

'I'll send in exactly $91,981.10,' I said. 'I'm keeping the $18.90 that Mrs. Stout owes me in library fines. And if First Fidelity is out of balance tonight, that's *their* problem!'

5

Still a Cop

Lieutenant Randall telephoned me on Tuesday, catching me in my cell-sized office at the public library just after I'd finished lunch.

'Hal?' he said. 'How come you're not out playing patty-cake with the book borrowers?' Randall still resents my leaving the police department to become a library detective — what he calls a 'sissy cop'. Nowadays my assignments — ostensibly — involve nothing more dangerous than tracing stolen and overdue books for the public library.

I said, 'Even a library cop has to eat, Lieutenant. What's on your mind?'

'Same old thing. Murder.'

'I haven't killed anyone for over a week,' I said.

His voice took on a definite chill. 'Somebody killed a young fellow we took out of the river this morning. Shot him through the head. And tortured him beforehand.'

'Sorry,' I said. I'd forgotten how grim it was to be a homicide cop. 'Tortured, did you say?'

'Yeah. Cigar burns all over him. I need information, Hal.'

'About what?'

'You ever hear of *The Damion Complex?*'

'Sure. It's the title of a spy novel published last year.'

'I thought it might be a book.' There was satisfaction in Randall's voice now. 'Next question: you have that book in the public library?'

'Of course. Couple of copies, probably.'

'Do they have different numbers or something to tell them apart?'

'Yes, they do. Why?'

'Find out for me if one of your library copies of *The Damion Complex* has this number on it, will you?' He paused and I could hear paper rustling. 'ES4187.'

'Right,' I said. 'I'll get back to you in ten minutes.' Then, struck by something familiar about the number, I said, 'No, wait, hold it a minute, Lieutenant.' I pulled out of my desk drawer the list of overdue library books I'd received the previous morning and checked it hurriedly. 'Bingo,' I said into the phone. 'I picked up that book with that very number yesterday morning. How about that? Do you want it?'

'I want it.'

'For what?'

'Evidence, maybe.'

'In your torture-murder case?'

He lost patience. 'Look, just get hold of the book for me, Hal. I'll tell you about it when I pick it up, okay?'

'Okay, Lieutenant. When?'

'Ten minutes.' He sounded eager.

I hung up and called Ellen on the checkout desk. 'Listen, sweetheart,' I said to her, because it makes her mad to be called 'sweetheart' and she's extremely attractive when she's mad, 'can you find me *The Damion Complex*, copy number ES4187? I brought it in yesterday among the overdues.'

'*The Damion Complex*?' She took

down the number. 'I'll call you back, Hal.' She didn't sound a bit mad. Maybe she was softening up at last. I'd asked her to marry me 17 times in the last six months, but she was still making up her mind.

In two minutes she called me back. 'It's out again,' she reported. 'It went out on card number 3888 yesterday after you brought it in.'

Lieutenant Randall was going to love that. 'Who is card number 3888?'

'A Miss Oradell Murphy.'

'Address?'

She gave it to me, an apartment on Leigh Street.

'Telephone number?'

'I thought you might be able to look that up yourself.' She was tart. 'I'm busy out here.'

'Thank you, sweetheart,' I said. 'Will you marry me?'

'Not now. I told you I'm busy.' She hung up. But she did it more gently than usual, it seemed to me. She *was* softening up. My spirits lifted.

Lieutenant Randall arrived in less than the promised ten minutes. 'Where is it?'

he asked, fixing me with his cat stare. He seemed too big to fit into my office. 'You got it for me?'

I shook my head. 'It went out again yesterday. Sorry.'

He grunted in disappointment, took a look at my spindly visitor's chair, and decided to remain standing. 'Who borrowed it?'

I told him Miss Oradell Murphy, apartment 3A at the Harrington Arms on Leigh Street.

'Thanks.' He tipped a hand and turned to leave.

'Wait a minute. Where you going, Lieutenant?'

'To get the book.'

'Those apartments at the Harrington Arms are efficiencies,' I said. 'Mostly occupied by single working women. So maybe Miss Murphy won't be home right now. Why not call first?'

He nodded. I picked up my phone and gave our switchboard girl Miss Murphy's telephone number. Randall fidgeted nervously.

'No answer,' the switchboard reported.

I grinned at Randall. 'See? Nobody home.'

'I need that book.' Randall sank into the spindly visitor's chair and sighed in frustration.

'You were going to tell me why.'

'Here's why.' He fished a damp crumpled bit of paper out of an envelope he took from his pocket. I reached for it. He held it away. 'Don't touch it,' he said. 'We found it on the kid we pulled from the river this morning. It's the only damn thing we did find on him. No wallet, no money, no identification, no clothing labels, no nothing. Except for this he was plucked as clean as a chicken. We figure it was overlooked. It was in the bottom of his shirt pocket.'

'What's it say?' I could see water-smeared writing.

He grinned unexpectedly, although his yellow eyes didn't seem to realize that the rest of his face was smiling. 'It says: *PL Damion Complex ES4187.*'

'That's all?'

'That's all.'

'Great bit of deduction, Lieutenant,' I

said. 'You figured the *PL* for public library?'

'All by myself.'

'So what's it mean?'

'How do I know till I get the damn book?' He sat erect and went on briskly, 'Who had the book before Miss Murphy?'

I consulted my overdue list from the day before. 'Gregory Hazzard. Desk clerk at the Starlight Motel on City Line. I picked up seven books and fines from him yesterday.'

The lieutenant was silent for a moment. Then, 'Give Miss Murphy another try, will you?'

She still didn't answer her phone.

Randall stood up. My chair creaked when he removed his weight. 'Let's go see this guy Hazzard.'

'Me, too?'

'You, too.' He gave me the fleeting grin again. 'You're mixed up in this, son.'

'I don't see how.'

'Your library owns the book. And you belong to the library. So move your tail.'

Gregory Hazzard was surprised to see me again so soon. He was a middle-aged skeleton, with a couple of pounds of skin and gristle fitted over his bones so tightly that he looked like the object of an anatomy lesson. His clothes hung on him — snappy men's wear on a scarecrow. 'You got all my overdue books yesterday,' he greeted me.

'I know, Mr. Hazzard. But my friend here wants to ask you about one of them.'

'Who's your friend?' He squinted at Randall.

'Lieutenant Randall, City Police.'

Hazzard blinked. 'Another cop? We went all through that with the boys from your robbery detail day before yesterday.'

Randall's eyes flickered, otherwise he didn't change expression. 'I'm not here about that. I'm interested in one of your library books.'

'Which one?'

'*The Damion Complex.*'

Hazzard bobbed his skull on his pipestem neck. 'That one. Just a so-so yarn. You can find better spy stories in your newspaper.'

Randall ignored that. 'You live here in the motel, Mr. Hazzard?'

'No. With my sister down the street a ways, in a duplex.'

'This is your address on the library records,' I broke in. 'The Starlight Motel.'

'Sure. Because this is where I read all the books I borrow. And where I work.'

'Don't you ever take library books home?' Randall asked.

'No. I leave 'em here, right at this end of the desk, out of the way. I read 'em during slack times, you know? When I finish 'em I take 'em back to the library and get another batch. I'm a fast reader.'

'But your library books were overdue. If you're such a fast reader, how come?'

'He was sick for three weeks,' I told Randall. 'Only got back to work Saturday.'

The lieutenant's lips tightened, and I knew from old experience that he wanted me to shut up. 'That right?' he asked Hazzard. 'You were sick?'

'As a dog. Thought I was dying. So'd my sister. That's why my books were overdue.'

'They were here on the desk all the time you were sick?'

'Right. Cost me a pretty penny in fines, too, I must say. Hey, Mr. Johnson?'

I laughed. 'Big deal. Two ninety-four, wasn't it?'

He chuckled so hard I thought I could hear his bones rattle. 'Cheapest pleasure we got left, free books from the public library.' He sobered suddenly. 'What's so important about *The Damion Complex*, Lieutenant?'

'Wish I knew.' Randall signaled me with his eyes. 'Thanks, Mr. Hazzard, you've been helpful. We'll be in touch.' He led the way out to the police car.

On the way back to town he turned aside ten blocks and drove to the Harrington Arms Apartments on Leigh Street. 'Maybe we'll get lucky,' he said as he pulled up at the curb. 'If Murphy's home, get the book from her, Hal, okay? No need to mention the police.'

A comely young lady, half out of a nurse's white uniform and evidently just home from work, answered my ring at apartment 3A. 'Yes?' she said, hiding her dishabille by standing behind the door and peering around its edge.

'Miss Oradell Murphy?'

'Yes.' She had a fetching way of raising her eyebrows.

I showed her my ID card and gave her a cock-and-bull story about *The Damion Complex* having been issued to her yesterday by mistake. 'The book should've been destroyed,' I said, 'because the previous borrower read it while she was ill with an infectious disease.'

'Oh,' Miss Murphy said. She gave me the book without further questions.

When I returned to the police car Lieutenant Randall said, 'Gimme,' and took the book from me, handling it with a finicky delicacy that seemed odd in such a big man. By his tightening lips I could follow his growing frustration as he examined *The Damion Complex*. For it certainly seemed to be just an ordinary copy of another ordinary book from the public library. The library name was stamped on it in the proper places. Identification number ES4187. Card pocket, with regulation date card, inside the front cover. Nothing concealed between its pages, not even a pressed forget-me-not.

'What the hell?' the lieutenant grunted.

'Code message?' I suggested.

He was contemptuous. 'Code message? You mean certain words off certain pages? In that case, why was this particular copy specified — number ES4187? Any copy would do.'

'Unless the message is in the book itself. In invisible ink? Or indicated by pin pricks over certain words?' I showed my teeth at him. 'After all, it's a spy novel.'

We went over the book carefully twice before we found the negative. And no wonder. It was very small — no more than half an inch or maybe five-eighths — and shoved deep in the pocket inside the front cover, behind the date card.

Randall held it up to the light. 'Too small to make out what it is,' I said. 'We need a magnifying glass.'

'Hell with that.' Randall threw his car into gear. 'I'll get Jerry to make me a blowup.' Jerry is the police photographer. 'I'll drop you off at the library.'

'Oh, no, Lieutenant. I'm mixed up in

this. You said so yourself. I'm sticking until I see what's on that negative.' He grunted.

Half an hour later I was in Randall's office at headquarters when the police photographer came in and threw a black-and-white $3\frac{1}{2}$ by $4\frac{1}{2}$ print on the Lieutenant's desk. Randall allowed me to look over his shoulder as he examined it.

Its quality was poor. It was grainy from enlargement, and the images were slightly blurred, as though the camera had been moved just as the picture was snapped. But it was plain enough so that you could make out two men sitting facing each other across a desk. One was facing the camera directly; the other showed only as part of a rear-view silhouette — head, right shoulder, right arm.

The right arm, however, extended into the light on the desk top and could be seen quite clearly. It was lifting from an open briefcase on the desk a transparent bag of white powder, about the size of a pound of sugar. The briefcase contained three more similar bags. The man who was full face to the camera was reaching out a hand to accept the bag of white powder.

Lieutenant Randall said nothing for what seemed a long time. Then all he did was grunt noncommittally.

I said, 'Heroin, Lieutenant?'

'Could be.'

'Big delivery. Who's the guy making the buy? Do you know?'

He shrugged. 'We'll find out.'

'When you do, you'll have your murderer. Isn't that what you're thinking?'

He shrugged again. 'How do you read it, Hal?'

'Easy. The kid you pulled from the river got this picture somehow, decided to cut himself in by a little blackmail, and got killed for his pains.'

'And tortured. Why tortured?' Randall was just using me as a sounding board.

'To force him to tell where the negative was hidden? He wouldn't have taken the negative with him when he braced the dope peddler.'

'Hell of a funny place to hide a negative,' Randall said. 'You got any ideas about that?'

I went around Randall's desk and sat down. 'I can guess. The kid sets up his blackmail meeting with the dope peddler, then starts out with both the negative and a print of it, like this one, to keep his date. At the last minute he has second thoughts about carrying the negative with him.'

'Where's he starting out from?' Randall squeezed his hands together.

'The Starlight Motel. Where else?'

'Go on.'

'So maybe he decides to leave the negative in the motel safe and stops at the desk in the lobby to do so. But Hazzard is in the can, maybe. Or has stepped out to the restaurant for coffee. The kid has no time to waste. So he shoves the little negative into one of Hazzard's library books temporarily, making a quick note of the book title and library number so he can find it again. You found the note in his shirt pocket. How's that sound?'

Randall gave me his half grin and said, 'So long, Hal. Thanks for helping.'

I stood up. 'I need a ride to the library. You've wasted my whole afternoon. You going to keep my library book?'

'For a while. But I'll be in touch.'

'You'd better be. Unless you want to pay a big overdue fine.'

★　★　★

It was the following evening before I heard any more from Lieutenant Randall. He telephoned me at home. 'Catch any big bad book thieves today, Hal?' he began in a friendly voice.

'No. You catch any murderers?'

'Not yet. But I'm working on it.'

I laughed. 'You're calling to report progress, is that it?'

'That's it.' He was as bland as milk.

'Proceed,' I said.

'We found out who the murdered kid was.'

'Who?'

'A reporter named Joel Homer from Cedar Falls. Worked for the *Cedar Falls Herald*. The editor tells me Homer was working on a special assignment the last few weeks. Trying to crack open a story on dope in the Tri-Cities.'

'Oho. Then it *is* dope in the picture.'

'Reasonable to think so, anyway.'

'How'd you find out about the kid? The Starlight Motel?'

'Yeah. Your friend Hazzard, the desk clerk, identified him for us. Remembered checking him into room 18 on Saturday morning. His overnight bag was still in the room and his car in the parking lot.'

'Well, it's nice to know who got killed,' I said, 'but you always told me you'd rather know who did the killing. Find out who the guy in the picture is?'

'He runs a ratty café on the river in Overbrook, just out of town. Name of Williams.'

'Did you tie up the robbery squeal Hazzard mentioned when we were out there yesterday?'

'Could be. One man, masked, held up the night clerk, got him to open the office safe, and cleaned it out. Nothing much in it, matter of fact — hundred bucks or so.'

'Looking for that little negative, you think?'

'Possibly, yeah.'

'Why don't you nail this Williams and find out?'

'On the strength of that picture?' Randall said. 'Uh-uh. That was enough to put him in a killing mood, maybe, but it's certainly not enough to convict him of murder. He could be buying a pound of sugar. No, I'm going to be sure of him before I take him.'

'How do you figure to make sure of him, for God's sake?'

I shouldn't have asked that, because as a result I found myself, two hours later, sitting across that same desk — the one in the snapshot — from Mr. Williams, suspected murderer. We were in a sizable back room in Williams's café in Overbrook. A window at the side of the room was open, but the cool weed-scented breeze off the river didn't keep me from sweating.

'You said on the phone you thought I might be interested in a snapshot you found,' Williams said. He was partially bald. Heavy black eyebrows met over his nose. The eyes under them looked like brown agate marbles in milk. He was smoking a fat cigar.

'That's right,' I said.

'Why?'

'I figured it could get you in trouble in certain quarters, that's all.'

He blew smoke. 'What do you mean by that?'

'It's actually a picture of you buying heroin across this desk right here. Or maybe selling it.'

'Well, well,' he said, 'that's interesting all right. If true.' He was either calm and cool or trying hard to appear so.

'It's true,' I said. 'You're very plain in the picture. So's the heroin.' I gave him the tentative smile of a timid, frightened man. It wasn't hard to do, because I felt both timid and frightened.

'Where is this picture of yours?' Williams asked.

'Right here.' I handed him the print Lieutenant Randall had given me.

He looked at it without any change of expression I could see. Finally he took another drag on his cigar. 'This guy does resemble me a little. But how did *you* happen to know that?'

I jerked a thumb over my shoulder. 'I been in your café lots of times. I recognized you.'

He studied the print. 'You're right about one thing. This picture might be misunderstood. So maybe we can deal. What I can't understand is where you found the damn thing.'

'In a book I borrowed from the public library.'

'A book?' He halted his cigar in midair, startled.

'Yes. A spy novel. I dropped the book accidentally and this picture fell out of the inside card pocket.' I put my hand into my jacket pocket and touched the butt of the pistol that Randall had issued me for the occasion. I needed comfort.

'You found this print in a book?'

'Not this print, no. I made it myself out of curiosity. I'm kind of an amateur photographer, see? When I found what I had, I thought maybe you might be interested, that's all. Are you?'

'How many prints did you make?'

'Just the one.'

'And where's the negative?'

133

'I've got it, don't worry.'

'With you?'

'You think I'm nuts?' I said defensively. I started a hand toward my hip pocket, then jerked it back nervously.

Mr. Williams smiled and blew cigar smoke. 'What do you think might be a fair price?' he asked.

I swallowed. 'Would twenty thousand dollars be too much?'

His eyes changed from brown marbles to white slits. 'That's pretty steep.'

'But you'll pay it?' I tried to put a touch of triumph into my expression.

'Fifteen. When you turn over the negative to me.'

'Okay,' I said, sighing with relief. 'How long will it take you to get the money?'

'No problem. I've got it right here when you're ready to deal.' His eyes went to a small safe in a corner of the room. Maybe the heroin was there, too, I thought.

'Hey!' I said. 'That's great, Mr. Williams! Because I've got the negative here, too. I was only kidding before.' I fitted my right hand around the gun butt in my pocket. With my left I pulled out my wallet and threw it on the desk between us.

'In here?' Williams said, opening the wallet.

'In the little pocket.'

He found the tiny negative at once.

He took a magnifying glass from his desk drawer and used it to look at the negative against the ceiling light. Then he nodded, satisfied. He raised his voice a little and said, 'Okay, Otto.'

Otto? I heard a door behind me scrape over the rug as it was thrust open. Turning in my chair, I saw a big man emerge from a closet and step toward me. My eyes went instantly to the gun in his hand. It was fitted with a silencer, and oddly, the man's right middle finger was curled around the trigger. Then I saw why. The tip of his right index finger was missing. The muzzle of the gun looked as big and dark as Mammoth Cave to me.

'He's all yours, Otto,' Williams said. 'I've got the negative. No wonder you couldn't find it in the motel safe. The crazy kid hid it in a library book.'

'I heard,' Otto said flatly.

I still had my hand in my pocket touching the pistol, but I realized I didn't have a chance of beating Otto to a shot, even if I shot through my pocket. I stood up very slowly and faced Otto. He stopped far enough away from me to be just out of reach.

Williams said, 'No blood in here this time, Otto. Take him out back. Don't forget his wallet and labels. And it won't hurt to spoil his face a little before you put him in the river. He's local.'

Otto kept his eyes on me. They were paler than his skin. He nodded. 'I'll handle it.'

'Right.' Williams started for the door that led to his cafe kitchen, giving me an utterly indifferent look as he went by. 'So long, smart boy,' he said. He went through the door and closed it behind him.

Otto cut his eyes to the left to make sure Williams had closed the door tight. I used that split second to dive headfirst over Williams's desk, my hand still in my pocket on my gun. I lit on the floor behind the desk with a painful thump, and Williams's desk chair, which I'd overturned in my plunge, came crashing down on top of me.

From the open window at the side of the room a new voice said conversationally, 'Drop the gun, Otto.'

Apparently Otto didn't drop it fast enough, because Lieutenant Randall shot it out of his hand before climbing through the window into the room. Two uniformed cops followed him.

* * *

Later, over a pizza and beer in the Trocadero All-Night Diner, Randall said, 'We could've taken Williams before. The Narc Squad has known for some time he's a peddler. But we didn't know who was supplying him.'

I said stiffly, 'I thought I was supposed to be trying to hang a murder on him. How did that Otto character get into the act?'

'After we set up your meeting with Williams, he phoned Otto to come over to his café and take care of another would-be blackmailer.'

'Are you telling me you didn't think Williams was the killer?'

Randall shook his head, looking slightly sheepish. 'I was pretty sure Williams wouldn't risk Murder One. Not when he had a headlock on somebody who'd do it for him.'

'Like Otto?'

'Like Otto.'

'Well, just who the hell *is* Otto?'

'He's the other man in the snapshot with Williams.'

Something in the way he said it made me ask him, 'You mean you knew who he was *before* you asked me to go through that charade tonight?'

'Sure. I recognized him in the picture.'

I stopped chewing my pizza and stared at him. I was dumfounded, as they say. 'Are you nuts?' I said with my mouth full. 'The picture just showed part of a silhouette. From behind, at that. Unrecognizable.'

'You didn't look close enough.' Randall gulped beer. 'His right hand showed in the picture plain. With the end of his right index finger gone.'

'But how could you recognize a man from that?'

'Easy. Otto Schmidt of our Narcotics Squad is missing the end of his right index finger. Had it shot off by a junkie in a raid.'

'There are maybe a hundred guys around with fingers like that. You must've had more to go on than that, Lieutenant.'

'I did. The heroin.'

'You recognized that, too?' I was sarcastic.

'Sure. It was the talk of the department a week ago, Hal.'

'What was?'

'The heroin. Somebody stole it right out of the Narc Squad's own safe at headquarters.' He laughed aloud. 'Can you believe it? Two kilos, packaged in four bags, just like in the picture.'

I said, 'How come it wasn't in the news?'

'You know why. It'd make us look pretty stupid.'

'Anyway, one bag of heroin looks just

like every other,' I said, unconvinced.

'You didn't see the *big* blowup I had made of that picture,' the lieutenant said. 'A little tag on one of the bags came out real clear. You could read it.'

All at once I felt very tired. 'Don't tell me,' I said.

He told me anyway, smiling. 'It said 'Confiscated, such and such a date, such and such a raid, by the Grandhaven Police Department.' That's us, Hal. Remember?'

I sighed. 'So you've turned up another crooked cop. Believe me, I'm glad I'm out of the business, Lieutenant.'

'You're *not* out of it.' Randall's voice roughened with some emotion I couldn't put a name to. 'You're still a cop, Hal.'

'I'm an employee of the Grandhaven Public Library.'

'Library fuzz. But still a cop.'

I shook my head.

'You helped me take a killer tonight, didn't you?'

'Yeah. Because you fed me a lot of jazz about needing somebody who didn't *smell* of cop. Somebody who knew the score but could act the part of a timid greedy citizen trying his hand at blackmail for the first time.'

'Otto Schmidt's a city cop. If I'd sent another city cop in there tonight, Otto would have recognized him immediately. That's why I asked you to go.'

'You could've told me the facts.'

He shook his head. 'Why? I thought you'd do better without knowing. And you did. The point is, though, that you *did* it. Helped me nail a killer at considerable risk to yourself. Even if the killer wasn't the one you thought. You didn't do it just for kicks, did you? Or because we found the negative in your library book, for God's sake?'

I shrugged and stood up to leave.

'So you see what I mean?' Lieutenant Randall said. 'You're still a cop.' He grinned at me. 'I'll get the check, Hal. And thanks for the help.'

I left without even saying good night. I could feel his yellow eyes on my back all the way out of the diner.

6

The Mutilated Scholar

I was standing in the rear of a crowded bus when I caught sight of the stolen library book. It was the wildest coincidence, the sheerest accident. Because I don't ride a bus even twice a year. And normally I can't tell one copy of a particular library book from another.

I craned my neck to get a clearer view past the fellow hanging to a bus strap beside me. And I knew immediately that I wasn't making any mistake. That library book tucked under the arm of the neatly dressed girl a few seats forward was, without a doubt, one of the 52 library books that had been in the trunk of my old car when it was stolen six weeks before. The police had recovered my car three days later. The books, however, were missing — until I spotted this one on the bus.

Maybe I'd better explain how I recognized it.

As a library cop, I run down overdue and stolen books for the public library. I'd been collecting overdues that day, and about eleven in the morning I'd got back a bunch of books from a wealthy old lady who'd borrowed them from the library to read on a round-the-world cruise. She couldn't have cared less when I told her how much money in fines she owed the library after ten weeks' delinquency. And she couldn't have cared less, either, when I taxed her with defacing one of the books.

It was a novel called *The Scholar*, and she'd deliberately — in an idle moment on the cruise, no doubt — made three separate burns on the cover with the end of her cigarette, to form two eyes and a nose inside the O of the word scholar. I was pretty irritated with her, because that sort of thing is in the same class with drawing mustaches on subway-poster faces, so I charged her two bucks for defacing the book in addition to the fine for overdue. You can see why I'd remember that particular copy of *The Scholar*.

I scrutinized the girl now holding it under her arm on the bus. She certainly didn't look like the kind of girl who goes around stealing old cars and public library books. She was maybe 30 years old, well-dressed in a casual way, with a pretty, high-cheekboned face and taffy-colored (dyed?) hair, stylishly coiffured.

A crowded bus wasn't exactly the best place to brace her about the book, nevertheless I began to squeeze my way toward her between the jammed passengers. I wanted to know about that book because I still winced every time I recalled the mirth of Lieutenant Randall of the police department when I called him that first day to report the theft of my car and books. First he had choked with honest laughter, then he accused me of stealing my own library books so I could make myself look good by finding them again, and finally he offered to bet I had sunk my car in the river somewhere so I could collect the insurance on it. The idea of a book detective being robbed of his own books sent him into paroxysms. It was understandable. I used to work for him, and he's always needled me about quitting the police to become a 'sissy' library cop.

The girl with the book was seated near the center doors of the bus. I managed to maneuver my way to a standing position in front of her, leaned over, and in a friendly voice said, 'Excuse me, miss. Would you mind telling me where you got that library book you're holding?'

Her head tilted back and she looked up at me, startled. 'What?' she said in a surprised contralto.

'That book,' I said, pointing to *The Scholar*. 'My name is Hal Johnson. I'm from the public library, and I wonder if you'd mind telling me where — '

That was as far as I got. She glanced out the window, pulled the cord to inform the bus driver of her desire to get off, and as she squeezed by me toward the center doors of the bus she said, 'Excuse me, this is my stop. This book is just one I got in the usual — '

The rest of what she said was lost in

the sound of the bus doors swishing open. The girl went lithely down the two steps to the sidewalk and made off at a brisk pace. I was too late to follow her out of the bus before the doors closed, but I prevailed on the driver to reopen them with some choice abuse about poor citizens who were carried blocks beyond their stops by insensitive bus drivers who didn't keep the doors open long enough for a fast cat to slip through them.

While I carried on my dispute with the bus driver, I'd kept my eye on the hurrying figure of the girl with *The Scholar* under her arm. So when I gained the sidewalk at last, I started out at a rapid trot in the direction she'd gone.

Being considerably longer-legged than she was, I was right behind her when she approached the revolving doors to Perry's Department Store. Whether or not she realized I was following her I didn't know. As she waited for an empty slot in the revolving door, a middle-aged, red-haired woman came out. She caught sight of my quarry and said in a hearty tone, loud enough for me to hear quite plainly,

'Why, hello, Gloria! You here for the dress sale too?'

Gloria mumbled something and was whisked into the store by the revolving door. I hesitated a moment, then stepped in front of the red-haired woman and said politely, 'That girl you just spoke to — the one you called Gloria — I'm sure I know her from somewhere.'

The red-haired woman grinned at me. 'I doubt it, buster,' she said, 'unless you get your hair styled at Heloise's Beauty Salon on the South Side. That's where Gloria works. She does my hair every Tuesday afternoon at three.'

'Oh,' I said. 'What's her last name, do you know?'

'I've no idea.' She sailed by me and breasted the waves of pedestrian traffic flowing past the store entrance. I went through the revolving door into Perry's and looked around anxiously. Gloria the hairdresser was nowhere in sight.

After a moment's survey of the five o'clock crowd jamming the store's aisles, I turned away. I was due to meet Susan for drinks and dinner at The Chanticleer in half an hour. And I figured Susan, whom I hoped to lure away from the checkout desk at the public library into marriage with me, was more important than a stolen copy of *The Scholar*. Especially since I now knew where to find Gloria and the stolen book.

★   ★   ★

Some of my pickups the next morning were on the South Side, so it wasn't out of my way to stop at Heloise's Beauty Salon. I went in, and, letting my eyes rove uneasily about the shop, feeling self-conscious, I asked at the reception counter if I could speak to Gloria for a minute.

'Gloria Dexter?' said the pretty receptionist. 'I'm afraid you can't. She's not here this morning.'

'Her day off?'

'No. Yesterday was her day off.'

'How come she's not here today?'

'We don't know. She just didn't show up. She usually calls in if she can't make it, but this morning she didn't.'

'Did you try telephoning her?' I asked. She nodded. 'No answer.'

'Well,' I said, 'maybe I can stop by her home. All I wanted to ask her about was a library book that's overdue. Where's she live?'

After I'd shown her my ID card, the receptionist told me Gloria Dexter's address. I thanked her and left.

The address wasn't fifteen minutes away. It turned out to be a single efficiency apartment perched on top of what used to be a small gatehouse to a private estate. The private estate was now two fourteen-story highrises set back from the street in shaded grounds. The only way up to Gloria's apartment was by a rusty outside stairway rather like a fire escape.

I was just starting up it when somebody behind me yelled, 'Hey!'

I stopped and turned around. The hail had come from a burly man in dirty slacks and a T-shirt who was clipping a hedge behind the gatehouse. 'No use going up there, mister,' he informed me, strolling over to the foot of Gloria's staircase. 'Miss Dexter isn't there.'

I'd been expecting that. I said, 'Do you know where she is?'

'At Memorial Hospital probably,' he replied, 'or the morgue. They took her off in an ambulance a couple of hours ago. I was the one who found her.'

I hadn't been expecting that. 'Did she have an accident or something?'

'She sure did. Fell all the way down that iron staircase you're standing on. Caved in her skull, it looked like to me.'

I assimilated this news in silence. Then, 'You found her at the bottom of this staircase?'

'Yep. Like a ragdoll.'

'What time?'

'Eight thirty this morning when I came to work. I'm the yardman here. The ambulance boys said she'd been dead for quite a while, so she musta taken her tumble last night sometime.'

Remembering the pretty receptionist at Heloise's Beauty Salon, I said, 'I stopped at the beauty shop where she works before I came here. They're worrying about her because she didn't show this morning. Maybe you ought to let them know.'

'Never thought of that. Who'd you say you were, mister?'

I showed him my ID card. 'I wanted to see Miss Dexter about an overdue library book,' I said. 'Say, could I go up and get the book out of her place now? It'll save the library a lot of bother later on.'

'Go ahead. On second thought, I'll come with you, to see you don't take nothing but your library book.' He grinned, exposing stained teeth. 'Besides, you can't get in her place 'less I let you in. It's locked.'

We climbed the rusty iron steps together. He unlocked the door at the top and we went into the Dexter apartment. It was as simple, pretty, and tasteful as Gloria herself. A daybed with a nubby red-and-gold coverlet stood against one wall, and over the bed there was a single hanging shelf filled with books.

I went straight to the bookshelf. 'The book I want should be here somewhere,' I said to the yardman. My eyes went down the row of spines. *The Scholar* wasn't

151

there. Neither were any of the other 51 library books that had been stolen with my car.

'Take a look in her kitchenette and bathroom,' the yardman advised me. 'People read books in funny places.'

A quick search failed to turn up *The Scholar* anywhere in the apartment.

The yardman was becoming impatient. 'Tough luck,' he said. 'I guess you'll have to wait for the book and get it the hard way.' He looked at the telephone on a dropleaf table near the kitchenette door. 'I'll call her beauty shop from here,' he said. 'It'll be handier.' He opened the telephone book, then hesitated. 'What's the name of the place, anyhow?' he asked me. 'Some fancy French name I can't remember.'

'I'll look it up for you,' I said. 'Heloise's Beauty Salon is what it's called. With an H.' I riffled through the telephone book and found the number for him. Another number on the same page was underlined in red. The yardman thanked me and I thanked him, and as I left, he was dialing the beauty shop.

My car was stifling when I climbed back into it. I rolled down the windows and sat for a couple of minutes, trying to figure out what to do next. Finally I drove downtown, left my car in the parking lot behind Perry's Department Store, and went inside.

At the lost and found counter I asked the girl, 'Has a public library book been turned in recently?'

She gave me a funny look and said, 'Yes, the clean-up crew found one in a trash basket.'

'Mine,' I said with relief. 'May I have it, please?'

'Can you describe it?' she said.

'Sure. The title is *The Scholar*. There are three cigarette burns inside the O on the cover. Like eyes and a nose.' When she looked prim I added, 'Somebody else put them there, not me.'

She was suddenly businesslike. 'That's the book, all right. But we don't have it here. You'll have to claim it at the security office.' She dropped her eyes. 'I turned it over to them a few minutes ago.'

'What did you do that for?' I asked curiously.

'Ask security,' she said. 'Mr. Helmut.'

'I will. Mr. Helmut. Where can I find him?'

She pointed toward the balcony that ran along one side of Perry's street floor. 'Up there. Behind the partitions.'

I mounted to the balcony and pushed open an opaque glass door with the words 'Security Office' stenciled on it. A girl with dull eyes behind horn-rimmed glasses was sitting at a desk inside the door, typing. She asked me what I wanted in a no-nonsense voice that didn't go with her bitten fingernails.

'You the security chief?' I asked, giving her my best smile.

'Don't be silly!' she answered sharply. 'Mr. Helmut is our security chief.'

'Then I'd like to see him for a minute, please.'

'He's out in the store making his morning round. Maybe I can help you?'

'Your lost and found desk sent me up here to ask about a book from the public library that was found in the store last night.'

She gave me a blank look. 'I'm sorry, I don't know anything about any library book. Mr. Helmut ought to be back soon if you'd care to wait.' She waved at one of those form-fitting chairs for which I understand the Swedes are responsible. I sat down in it.

Ten minutes later a burly black-browed man with long sideburns pushed open the security door and came in. He paused abruptly when he saw me. He had my stolen copy of *The Scholar* in his hand.

'Mr. Helmut,' his secretary fluted, 'this gentleman is waiting to see you about a library book.'

He shot me a sharp glance out of quick intelligent brown eyes and said, 'Okay. Come on in.' He held the door to his private office open and I preceded him inside. He motioned me to a straight chair and sat down behind a desk bearing a small metal sign that read 'C. B. Helmut'. He put my library book on the desk top and raised his black eyebrows at me.

'A library book?' he inquired. 'This one?' He pointed at *The Scholar*.

I nodded. 'That's the one. It was stolen from me some time ago, Mr. Helmut. The reason I'm here is that yesterday, on a bus, I saw a girl carrying it under her arm. I recognized it by those burns on the cover. When I tried to ask the girl about it, she ducked into your store — maybe to brush me off in the crowd of shoppers, or maybe to get rid of the stolen book before anybody caught her with it.'

'The clean-up crew found it in a trash basket here last night,' Helmut said.

'So your lost and found girl told me. She also told me the book was turned over to her first. Then she turned it over to you. Mind telling me why?'

'Routine security measure, that's all.' Helmut ran a thick finger over the cigarette burns on the cover of *The Scholar*. He was enjoying himself, acting the important executive.

'Security measure?' I said. 'How does store security come into it?'

Idly he opened the cover of *The Scholar* and leafed through the first 20 pages or so in a leisurely manner, wetting his fingertip to turn the pages. Then suddenly he said, 'Look here, Mr. Johnson,' and held out the opened book for my inspection. *The Scholar* was a 400-page book, more than two inches thick. The copy Helmut held out to me was only a dummy book. The insides had been cut out to within half an inch of each edge, so that the book was now, in effect, an empty box, its covers and the few pages left intact at front and back concealing a cavity about seven inches long, four wide, and an inch and a half deep.

I said, 'So that's it.'

'That's it.' Helmut echoed me. 'A shoplifting gimmick. You see how it works? Shoplifter comes into the store, puts down her library book on the counter while she examines merchandise, and when our salesclerk isn't looking, the shoplifter merely opens the book and pops in a wristwatch or a diamond pin or a couple of lipsticks or whatever and walks out with them, cool as you please.' Helmut shook his head in reluctant admiration. 'Can you imagine a more innocent-looking hiding place for stolen goods than a public library book? Why, it even lends class to the shoplifter; gives her literary respectability.'

'Shoplifting!' was all I could think of to say.

'Pilferage ran almost a million bucks in this store last year,' Helmut went on. 'Most of it shoplifting. So we're pretty well onto the usual dodges — shopping bags with false bottoms, loose coats with big inside pockets, girls leaving fitting rooms with three or four sweaters under the one they wore going in, and so on. But this library-book trick is a new one on me. And it's a beaut!'

It was a beaut all right. I said, 'You better watch out for more of the same, Mr. Helmut. Because that girl stole fifty-one other library books when she stole this one. Out of my car.'

'Ouch!' he said. Then, 'You're from the public library?'

I nodded and showed him my card.

'Well,' said Helmut, 'since you scared her yesterday, let's hope she'll think twice about using the library-book method again.'

'Let's hope so. Can I have the book now?'

'Sure,' he said. He handed me the book.

'I wish I hadn't lost the girl last evening,' I said. 'I might have gotten my other books back too.'

'Wouldn't do you much good if she's gutted them all like that one,' Helmut said as I went out.

* * *

At two o'clock I was sitting across a scarred desk from Lieutenant Randall, my old boss. I'd just related to him in detail my adventures in recovering *The Scholar*, now considerably the worse for wear. The book lay on his desk between us.

Randall put his cat-yellow eyes on me and said, 'I'm very happy for you, Hal, that you managed to recover a stolen book for your little old library. Naturally. But why tell me about it? Petty book theft just doesn't interest me.' He was bland.

I gave him a grin and said, 'How about first-degree murder, Lieutenant? Could you work up any interest in that?'

He sat forward in his chair. It creaked under his weight. 'You mean the Dexter woman?'

I nodded. 'I think she was killed because I spotted her with my stolen book.'

'She fell downstairs and fractured her skull. You just said so.'

'She fell downstairs, all right. But I think she was pushed. After somebody had caved in her skull in her apartment.'

'Nuts,' Randall said. 'You're dreaming.'

'Call the coroner,' I suggested. 'If the dent in her head was made by hitting one of those rusty iron steps, there could be some rust flakes in the wound. But I'll bet there aren't any.'

'Jake hasn't looked at her yet. She only came in this morning. I've seen the preliminary report — fatal accident, no suspicion of foul play.'

'Ask him to take a look at her now, then.'

'Not until you give me something more

to go on than rust flakes.' He laced his voice with acid. 'You're a showoff, Hal. So you probably think you know who killed her, right? *If* she was killed.'

'Mr. C. B. Helmut,' I said. 'The security chief at Perry's Department Store. That's who killed her.'

Randall's unblinking yellow stare didn't shift. 'What makes you think it was Helmut?'

'Three pieces of what I consider solid evidence.'

'Such as?'

'Number One: when I looked up the phone number of Heloise's Beauty Salon for the yardman in Gloria Dexter's phone book, there was another number on the same page underlined in red ink.'

Randall frowned. 'Helmut's?'

'C. B. Helmut.'

'If she was a shoplifter,' Randall said, 'why the hell did she want to know the phone number of Perry's security chief?'

'Especially,' I said, 'since the underlined phone number was Helmut's *home* number, not the extension for security at Perry's Department Store.'

Randall's knuckles cracked as he curled his hands into fists. 'What's evidence Number Two?' he asked in a neutral tone.

'Helmut called me by name, although I was a perfect stranger to him and him to me.'

Randall said, 'Why not? You showed him your ID card.'

'He called me Mr. Johnson before he saw my ID card.'

'The lost and found girl or his secretary told him who you were.'

'I didn't tell either one of them my name.'

'Well.' Randall stared past my shoulder in deep thought. 'He knew who you were and what your job was before you told him, then?'

'Yes. And there can be only one explanation for that.'

'Don't tell me. Let me guess. You think he stole your car and your books.'

'Right. I'm sure he recognized me the minute he saw me today.'

'I don't see what the hell that has to do with Dexter's murder.'

'Dexter was in cahoots with Helmut,' I said. 'She told him I followed her and chased her into the store.'

'Wait a minute,' Randall said. 'You've lost me.'

I laid it out for him. 'The girl was scared when I braced her about the library book. She ducks into Perry's to lose me, but has the bad luck to meet one of her hairdressing customers at the entrance. From inside the door she looks back and sees that I've stopped her customer and am obviously asking about her, about Dexter. So she panics. She steps into one of the store telephone booths, gets Helmut on the phone, and tells him a Hal Johnson from the public library is hot on her trail and by now probably knows who she is on account of the hairdressing customer. What should she do?

'Helmut tells her not to come near the security office, just throw the library book into a trash basket and go on home. And deny she ever had the book if anybody asks her again about it. Helmut hopes the book will be burned in the store incinerator with the other trash, of course. But the book is turned in to the lost and found desk this morning, so Helmut's stuck with it. And I show up before he can dispose of it.'

'You should've been a detective,' Randall said, deadpan. 'I still don't see how that gets Dexter murdered.'

'Helmut knows I'll get to Dexter sooner or later, now that I know who she is. He knows I'll apply pressure about the stolen book and eventually go to the police. So he figures she'll blow the whole sweet setup he's got going for him, unless he takes her out of the picture completely.'

'What setup?'

'Don't you get it? The guy's a modern Fagan,' I said. 'He's got a bunch of girls like Dexter shoplifting for him all over town! Using scooped-out library books — the books he stole from me — as containers. And reporting to him by telephone at home.'

Randall took that without blinking. 'Well, well,' he murmured. He contemplated his folded hands on the desktop.

'You said something about a third piece of evidence?'

I gave him a sheepish look. 'I hesitate to tell you about that one. It's slightly illegal.'

'So is your friend Helmut, you think. So tell me.'

'I talked my way past Helmut's super and got into his apartment at Highland Towers.'

Randall blinked at last. 'And — ?' he said.

'I found twenty-seven of my stolen library books at the back of his clothes closet.'

'Scooped out?'

I shook my head. 'No, perfectly normal.'

'So.' Lieutenant Randall leaned back and put his hands behind his head, his elbows spread. 'Twenty-seven, you said? You think he's got people using the other twenty-five books in shoplifting for him?'

I nodded.

'That he's recruited a gang of otherwise respectable people like Dexter to turn shoplifter for him?'

I nodded again.

Randall ruminated aloud. 'He's store security chief. In the course of his job he runs into a lot of people who are *already* shoplifters, is that what you mean? So he blackmails some of them into working for him by threatening them with the police?'

'It could be, couldn't it?'

Randall looked at me with the air of a man who suspects his son of cheating on a geography exam. 'Hal,' he said, 'you recently remarked, and I quote: 'The guy's a modern Fagan. He's got a bunch of girls shoplifting' et cetera.' He tapped his desk top with a finger like a sausage. 'How do you know they're *all* girls? You holding out something else?'

'I found a list of girls' names in one of the stolen library books in Helmut's place. Here's a copy.' I tossed an old envelope on his desk.

He made no move to touch it. 'That isn't evidence, Hal. It could be a list of his daughter's friends. Members of his wife's bridge club. Anything.'

I said. 'I *know* one of the girls on that list, Lieutenant. Ramona Gomez — she works in the library cafeteria. Couldn't you go and ask her in a friendly way if she's been blackmailed into shoplifting for Helmut? With what you know now, it shouldn't be hard to make her talk.'

Randall stood up. 'Yeah,' he grunted, 'I guess I could do that much, Hal. And a couple of other things too. Leave the book, will you?'

'Let me know how you make out,' I said, 'because the books in Helmut's closet still belong to the library, you know.'

★ ★ ★

I was at home having a lonely shot of Scotch after my delicious TV dinner when Lieutenant Randall phoned. Seven hours. He was a fast worker.

'How's the stolen library-book business?' he asked by way of greeting.

'Booming,' I replied. 'And how's it with the brave boys of Homicide?'

'Also,' he said. 'We've got your pal Helmut.'

'For Murder One?'

'What else? That print we turned up under the dash of your stolen car, remember? It's Helmut's.'

'Good,' I said. 'Does it match anything else?'

'Strange you should ask. It matches a thumbprint on the metal buckle of Dexter's dress. I guess Helmut dragged her to the iron stairway by the belt after he conked her.'

'No rust flakes in her head wound?'

'None.'

'What'd he conk her with?'

'Swedish ashtray. Glass. Hers. Weighs about two pounds. A perfect blunt instrument. His prints are on that too.'

'Careless, wasn't he?'

'You might say so. He failed to reckon with the brilliance of the police is how I'd put it.'

'You talked to Ramona Gomez?'

'Yep. We couldn't turn her off when we hinted that Helmut had knocked off Dexter. She spilled everything. Helmut caught her shoplifting at Perry's and blackmailed her into working for him, just as you figured. Same with the other girls.'

'Poor Ramona,' I said. 'You're not going to take any action against her, are you?'

'Immunity,' said Randall wryly, 'in exchange for her memoirs about Helmut. Same with all the girls on the list.'

I sipped my whiskey and asked, 'Did Ramona say anything about fingering me to Helmut?'

'Yeah. She admitted telling Helmut he could get a whole load of books from the public library without any chance of their being traced if he just swiped your car when you had the trunk filled with overdues.' Randall chuckled. 'Your Ramona pointed you out to Helmut as a prime source for library books when he got his big idea about using them for shoplifting.'

'That wasn't nice of Ramona,' I said. 'Maybe you better charge her with conspiracy or something, after all.'

'We only picked up Helmut half an hour ago,' Randall said. 'He was taking a briefcase full of stolen goodies to the fence he's been using. We trailed him to the fence before we jumped him, and got the fence too. Isn't that clever?'

'Brilliant,' I said. 'Who's the fence? Anybody I know?'

'None of your business. You're a book detective, remember? Fences are for adult cops, my boy.'

'As a book detective, then, I'm interested in whether any more of the library's books will turn up as shoplifters' tools,' I said. 'Bad for the library's image — you can understand that, Lieutenant.'

'Don't fret yourself, Hal. Helmut called all his girls last night after killing Dexter and instructed them to discontinue using library books in their work. At least, that's what all the girls have told us.'

'That means the library's lost twenty-five books, Lieutenant. Who wants to read a scooped-out novel, even for free? But you got the other twenty-seven for me, didn't you, out of Helmut's closet?'

'Evidence,' said Randall. 'You'll get them back after Helmut's trial.'

'What!' I yelled. 'That'll be months, maybe years!'

Randall sounded hurt. 'You've got nobody but yourself to thank for that,' he said. 'If you're going to solve my murders, you can't blame me for collecting your library books.'

7

The Savonarola Syndrome

Chapter 1

Monday noon, when I got back to my office at the library, there was a note on my desk. 'I'd like to see you when you have a minute,' it said. It was signed 'Ellen'.

Anytime Ellen wants to see me, I have a minute. She's the girl on the check-out desk at the library. She has a face like a Botticelli angel and a figure like an Egyptian belly-dancer.

I didn't even sit down at my desk. I went down the corridor to the main library room, turned in through the double doors, and walked over to Ellen's desk with what is sometimes referred to as a spring in my stride. I waited until she had checked out a dozen books for a lantern-jawed, grizzled old man whose taste, judging from his book titles, seemed to run to the care and feeding of tropical plants. Then I stepped up to her desk and said, 'Don't tell me, Ellen. Let me guess. You've decided to marry me.'

She smiled and shook her head. 'Don't nag me, Hal,' she said. 'I'm still thinking it over.'

'You've been thinking it over for four months and eight days now.' Which was true. 'And I've only asked for an answer six times. Or is it seven? Do you call that nagging?'

'Borderline case, I'd say. Anyway, that isn't what I wanted to see you about. This is a professional matter.'

Professional. That seemed an odd word to apply to my job. I'm the guy who chases down stolen and overdue books for the public library. Library fuzz. A kind of sissy cop. It's not exciting work, usually, but it's steady. And I suppose you *could* call it a profession of sorts. It pays a fair salary anyway — enough to marry Ellen on if she'd ever make up her mind to say 'yes'.

I said, 'What is this professional matter

that concerns you?'

'What it is,' Ellen said, 'is that there's something funny going on around here.'

'Tell your favorite detective all about it.'

'Somebody's stealing books from my current fiction rack.'

'What gives you that idea?'

'Well, a lot of people keep coming in and asking for *Cult of Venus*, and complaining to me because they can't ever find a copy of it on the shelves. It's that novel by Joel Carstairs — '

'Whee!' I interrupted her. 'That *Cult of Venus* book is a very warm item, baby. Have you read it?'

She flushed. 'What difference does that make? Until this morning, I've just taken it for granted that all our copies of the book are out, and that's why there aren't any on the shelves recently. It's a very popular book, of course. A bestseller.'

'Bound to be,' I teased her, 'what with all decency thrown to the winds, explicit scenes of wild sexual abandon every other page and — '

'Be serious, Hal! I'm trying to tell you that this morning, after three more requests for the book, I decided to check our records on it.'

'How many copies are we circulating?'

'Sixteen. Eight here and two each for our branches.' She brushed her hair back from her cheek. 'That's when I found something funny, when I checked the cards. Our records show that seven copies should be on the shelves. But they aren't. And they haven't been misfiled, either. I checked that. They've just disappeared, Hal. Don't you think that's funny?'

'Sure,' I said. 'Hilarious. Seven out of eight? That's a lot of copies for anyone to want of the same book. Even a dirty one.'

'It's not really dirty so much,' Ellen said primly, 'as frank and realistic.'

'Dirty,' I said. 'I read it.' I thought for a moment. An acne-splotched teenager approached Ellen's desk with an armload of books. I said, 'Here comes a customer, Ellen. I'll see what I can figure and see you later.'

I went back to my cubby-hole behind the office of the library's business manager, sat down at my desk, pulled over my telephone and made four quick calls to our branch libraries. In each case, I asked the librarian to check on the two copies of *Cult of Venus* her branch was circulating, and get back to me as soon as possible.

Twenty minutes later I had reports from all four branches. Of the eight copies of *Cult of Venus* assigned to the branches, only three were accounted for as out on loan. The other five had been returned by borrowers and should have been on the current fiction shelves waiting to go out again. But they weren't. They had disappeared without the slightest trace.

Digesting that little nugget of information, I stood up and prowled around my closet-sized office for a couple of minutes before walking down the hall to visit Ellen again.

'Listen,' I said to her when she was free for a minute, 'is that the dirtiest book we're circulating right now? The *Cult of Venus?*'

She said, 'Well, that's fairly outspoken all right, Hal, but . . . '

'We've got dirtier ones?'

She hesitated. 'For my money, *The Parallel Triangle* is about as dirty as you can get — to use your word.'

'You read that one, too?'

'Just skimmed it. Part of my job.' She made a *moue* of distaste.

'Then check out our copies of *The Parallel Triangle* for me, will you, Ellen? When you get a few minutes free?'

She looked at me with raised eyebrows. 'You think we've got some nutty thief here who loves dirty books?' she asked. 'Somebody who's so enthusiastic that he collects all the copies he can get?'

'It's a possibility. Let me know what you find out, anyway. And you might take a look at your records on a few other dirty books, too, while you're at it. Even any you think are only frank and realistic.'

Ellen sighed. 'Okay, Hal.'

I descended into the basement and grabbed a quick bite at the library cafeteria before setting out on my afternoon round of calls for overdue books and fines. When I returned to the library again at 5:30, Ellen had left for the day but there was another note on my desk. This one read:

The Parallel Triangle: Of our twelve copies, seven are missing. *Harrigan's Bag* (also very frank and realistic!): four of our eight are missing. How about that, Sherlock?

How about it, indeed?

Chapter 2

The next morning, I checked our branches on their copies of *The Parallel Triangle* and *Harrigan's Bag*. More than half of the branch library copies were missing. They'd disappeared without a trace. As Ellen had said, something very funny seemed to be going on.

In my six years at the public library, I've had plenty of experience with book thieves. They come in all shapes and sizes. People who steal library books for the few dollars they'll bring from unscrupulous secondhand book dealers. Poor people who steal library books because they truly love books, feel compelled to own them, and can't afford to buy them.

People who steal books just for the hell of it — sometimes to satisfy the urgings of deep-buried kleptomania, sometimes for no reason at all except the thrill of stealing.

Then there are the otherwise respectable book collectors who steal out-of-print, rare, hard-to-get books and special editions from the public library just to round out their collections.

And of course, there's a small but select group of secret pornography-lovers who steal salacious books from the library because they're ashamed to be seen openly buying or borrowing them.

Our current thief seemed to fit nicely into the latter category, judging by the type of books he was stealing. Yet if so, why would he want so many copies of each book? Even the most enthusiastic porno buff could only read one book at a time.

No, I decided, the thief I was after wasn't a secret lover of pornography. He had to be a market-wise practical thief who was conforming smartly to the law of supply and demand, interested only in the commercial benefits of his thievery.

For while our dirty books remained on the bestseller lists, it figured that public demand for them would expand constantly. Therefore the secondhand dealers could resell as many copies of these particular titles as they could lay their hands on. And quite probably, they'd pay our thief a considerably higher price for his stolen goods than ordinary books would bring.

Well, good for you, Johnson, I told myself. You've figured out why the books are being stolen. So now figure out who is stealing them and how to get them back. That's what the library is paying you for, after all. Those books go for anywhere up to eight ninety-five retail, and that adds up to a lot of scarce library dough. So what are you going to do about it?

Simple, I answered myself. I'll set a little trap for the rascal.

I requested that all our remaining copies of *The Parallel Triangle* be withdrawn from circulation when they were returned by borrowers, and sent to me at the main library. As the lewdest and most popular book of the lot, that title would make the best bait, I figured.

When I had a reasonable backlog of copies, I would feed one copy at a time onto the current fiction rack at the main library and sit nearby, personally, and watch what happened to it. If a legitimate borrower selected the book and checked it out at Ellen's desk in the regular way, I would put another copy on the rack and watch *that*. If anybody smuggled *The Parallel Triangle* out of the library without checking it out at Ellen's desk, I figured the chances would be good that I'd caught our thief in the act.

By Thursday morning enough copies of the book had come in to my office to provide continuing bait for a couple of days, I hoped — at least during the heavy traffic hours in the library when the thief might be expected to operate.

It might take weeks to land him, I realized. On the other hand, I could get lucky in an hour. With no copies of the book available now at any of our branches, the thief would be forced to patronize the main library if he wanted to snag any more copies of *The Parallel Triangle*.

I decided to start the action. Not that I expected much action in the true sense of the word. I foresaw weary hours of sitting on a hard chair in a distant corner of the reading room, watching my bait in the fiction rack. Yet it was a welcome relief from collecting overdue books and fines.

So about eleven o'clock Thursday morning, I salted the rack with one copy of *The Parallel Triangle* and took up my vigil. It was really quite pleasant, I discovered, because I could see Ellen's desk, and Ellen herself, from my spy-chair. And I didn't know of any better way to rest tired eyes than to look at Ellen.

As it turned out, the third customer who picked *The Parallel Triangle* from the rack was my man. Out of the busy noon-hour crowd of library habitués who were browsing through the stacks, scanning the card catalog files, lining up before the checkout and check-in desks, he suddenly appeared at quarter after twelve, sidling up to the current fiction shelf so casually as to make it seem almost accidental. Yet there was nothing accidental in the swiftness with which he plucked *The Parallel Triangle*, along with its nearest neighbor, from the rack, after only half-a-second's inspection of the shelf's contents.

With a nod of satisfaction he came at a brisk, decisive pace toward the reading room, where I was pretending to peruse a month-old issue of *National Geographic*. As he passed me, I got a good look at him over my magazine. He was medium tall, strongly built, and stooped a little with age but not much. His abundant shock of carefully combed hair was pure white. He wore rimless eyeglasses. Deep-graven lines bracketed his thin-lipped mouth. And the reddish-brown eyes, under brows that still retained some of the brown his hair coloring lost, held a curious half-desperate, half-resigned expression.

Altogether he was quite distinguished-looking. I couldn't easily imagine anyone looking less like a petty book thief. Yet there he was, two library books from the current fiction shelf in one hand, a black leather briefcase in the other. The leather briefcase looked expensive. So did the blue-checked slacks and navy blazer he was wearing.

He sat down in a vacant chair at one of the long reading-room tables and placed his briefcase on the table in front of him. Then he made a quiet business of reading the jacket-blurbs of *The Parallel Triangle* and leafing through it as though making up his mind whether he wanted to read it or not.

After five minutes of this, he raised his eyes without lifting his head, checked the other occupants of the reading room to make sure we were all absorbed in our books or magazines, then quietly lifted the lid of his briefcase three inches and slid *The Parallel Triangle* inside.

It was done as skillfully as a prestidigitator palms a card. One second *The Parallel Triangle* was there, resting on top of his briefcase; the next, it had disappeared, and the white-haired gentleman was examining the second library book he had selected from the rack.

At length he rose from his chair, took

his briefcase from the table, walked briskly into the main room and returned the second book to the fiction rack as though he had decided not to borrow it after all. He glanced briefly at Ellen's check-out desk and saw that her attention was fully occupied by the half-dozen people waiting in line at her desk. Immediately he swung about and walked confidently out the rear door of the main library room, which led down a short corridor to our technology department. The technology department has an entrance of its own from the street bordering the rear of the library.

I tossed aside my *National Geographic* and went right after him.

Chapter 3

He disappeared down one of the narrow passages in the technology department between the ceiling-high shelves of books. I let him go and made for the librarian on the desk. She was a friend of Ellen's, and quite bored enough to exchange idle chat with anybody who came along — even me. Her name is Laura.

Laura and I had covered her health, mine, Ellen's, the Oscar awards on TV last week, and were just getting to the prospects for our local baseball club when my distinguished-looking thief, swinging his briefcase jauntily, appeared from the maze of bookshelves. He cast a pleasant nod in our direction as he passed us before sauntering nonchalantly out the rear door of the library to the sidewalk.

I said, 'You know that old bird, Laura?'

She nodded. 'He's a steady customer. Comes here several times a week. He's a dear.'

'Interested in science and technology, is he?'

'Of course. He's retired now, but he used to be a professor of electrical engineering at the university.'

'Well, well,' I said. I decided it wouldn't be necessary to follow him any further right now. 'What's his name, do you know?'

'Dr. Amos Satchell. Doctor, as in Ph.D., not medicine.'

'And why does he come to your technology department so often if he's retired?'

'He's still writing books,' Laura said. 'He has a lot of research to do for them, naturally.'

'I see,' I said. But I didn't.

'Textbooks,' Laura went on. 'We have two or three of them here in the library, as a matter of fact.' She squinted at me. 'Why are you so curious about Dr. Satchell, Hal?'

I was tempted to answer her by advising her to check her shelves to see how many technical works on sexual subjects were missing, but decided against it. Instead I said, 'Just curious,' and left her, returning to my own office.

There wasn't any great rush now. I knew the identity of the thief, and I could get his address from his library card if he had one, or from the telephone book for that matter. And I wanted to think about Dr. Amos Satchell for a bit before I braced him.

So it wasn't until the next morning that I drove my old Chevy out City Line toward the university and pulled up in front of a small but neatly kept frame house, standing modestly well back from the street in a large lot, shielded from its nearest neighbors by high hedges. The professor liked his privacy, apparently.

I left the Chevy parked in the street before Professor Satchell's house and walked up the long path of stepping stones, parallel to his gravel driveway that led to his front door. I pressed the doorbell. Faintly I could hear musical chimes inside, announcing my arrival.

I was earnestly hoping the professor himself would be at home and that I wouldn't have to deal with a loyal wife or daughter or son. It's not my idea of fun to inform a nice woman that her husband or father is a dirty-minded old man who steals sexy books from the public library, if you know what I mean.

I needn't have worried. Dr. Amos Satchell himself opened the door to me, his thick white hair as smooth and neatly kept as his lawn and shrubbery outside. I felt suddenly unsure of myself. This venerable, respectable-looking retired scientist *couldn't* be a book thief. I'd made a mistake somewhere. To cover my embarrassment I said, 'Are you Dr. Amos Satchell?' I almost added a 'sir'. He was that kind of a guy.

He smiled cordially and nodded. 'What can I do for you?'

I cleared my throat. 'May I talk with you for a few minutes, Dr. Satchell? Alone?' I was still thinking about the possibility of a loving wife hovering around.

'Of course,' he said easily. He stepped back and held the door open, inviting me in. I thought that was a trifle odd, asking a stranger to come in, until I remembered that he'd probably noticed me talking to Laura, the librarian, yesterday.

Just for the record, though, I got out my identification card and showed it to him. 'I'm from the public library,' I said. He peered at my ID through his rimless bifocals.

'Ah, yes. Mr. Johnson, is it? Come in, won't you?'

He led me through a center hall, richly

carpeted, and into a small den, book-lined and cozy. I looked for copies of our stolen books among his volumes, but failed to locate any. He waved me to an easy chair and sat down himself behind a beautifully made desk of dark satiny wood. 'I've rather been expecting you, Mr. Johnson,' he said, 'since yesterday afternoon.' So he *had* recognized me.

I didn't say anything for a second or two. At that moment I was disliking my job intensely; I was reluctant to harry this harmless old fellow. At length I murmured, 'I'm afraid I've come on a rather unpleasant errand, Dr. Satchell.'

He went right on smiling. 'It's about the books I've stolen from your library, isn't it?'

I swallowed. 'That's right. You've . . . ah . . . appropriated quite a few of them, haven't you?'

He seemed to be making a mental calculation. 'A good many, it's true. But only a few titles.' No apology in his voice, no shame, no guilt, just a quiet statement of fact.

'*Cult of Venus*,' I said, '*The Parallel*

Triangle, Harrigan's Bag.'

Gravely he nodded his white-maned head. 'Those are the ones, yes.'

'Why did you confine yourself to those three titles? And why steal so many copies of each?'

'Because those three books are the latest and most blatant examples of the filth that is being foisted on us in the name of literature today!'

Satchell wasn't smiling now. His voice was sharp and high with angry passion. 'I consider it immoral and disgraceful that a great public institution like the library should pander to the lowest tastes; should offer a free reading of lewd and obscene books to the citizens of this city!'

So. A crusader. That's what Dr. Satchell was. I remembered Ellen's guess that our thief might be a nut who loved dirty books. He wasn't, obviously. He was a nut who *hated* dirty books. I said, 'What good did you think you could do by stealing those few books from the library?'

'I hoped I could get them all, Mr. Johnson, before I was apprehended. Get at least those three disgusting books off the shelves where teenagers — and yes, even children — are exposed to their insidious corrupting influence! I stole them as a protest, I suppose. Against the careless, pernicious, permissive book selections made by our library board. In the hope that future selections might be more seemly and decent than those abominations I have stolen!'

Quite a speech. Dr. Satchell sank back in his chair. I said, as soothingly as I could, 'You're absolutely right, Dr. Satchell. Some of the material our writers are turning out today is garbage of the worst kind. But surely you couldn't have hoped to do much to turn the tide of what you call 'filth' by stealing only a few books from the public library?'

He ran a thin hand across his forehead, puzzled and distraught. 'I don't know,' he said vaguely. 'I don't know. Perhaps I *was* foolish to think I could accomplish anything in such a fashion. I . . . I realize that now . . . '

I interrupted him. 'In that case,' I said, 'maybe we can make a deal, sir.' I was feeling very sorry for the troubled old gentleman. And my own sympathies, I must admit, leaned toward his view of current fiction. 'The library has no desire to be unduly harsh about your book stealing, Dr. Satchell. To a certain extent, we can understand and sympathize with your views.'

I took a list from my pocket and held it out to him. He made no move to take it. 'As nearly as we can figure it, these are the books you've stolen from us. If you're willing to return them now, and pay a fine of ten cents per day per book for the period you've kept them, I think we can arrange to settle the matter without recourse to the police.' I was struck by a sudden thought. 'You haven't destroyed the books, have you?'

Dr. Satchell shook his head. 'Oh, no. Not yet. I intended to gather them all together and burn them publicly in Woodhouse Square, as Savonarola did in Florence long ago. But I fully realize now that that would be an exercise in futility.'

'Good,' I said. 'Then you'll return the books and pay the fine?

He sighed. 'Rather than go to prison, yes, of course. I need my freedom to carry on the work, Mr. Johnson. I do not admit defeat, you understand. I merely realize that sterner measures will be required to dam the flow of prurient material you peddle to the public.' He stood up and turned toward a door in the corner of the den. 'Your library books are here,' he said. 'I've kept them in my closet, out of sight. You can understand why.'

I nodded and crossed the room to join him as he opened the closet door.

'There they are, on the floor, Mr. Johnson.'

It was dark in the closet. I stepped past him and stooped in the doorway, reaching out my hands for the books, and feeling a wave of relief that we wouldn't have to get tough, after all, with poor old Dr. Satchell, since he had turned out to be merely a pathetic crank and not a real criminal at all.

Poor old pathetic Dr. Satchell. I don't know what he hit me with. Later I figured it might have been a heavy onyx ashtray I'd noticed on his desk. But hit me he did

— a good solid belt on the back of the head that tumbled me into the closet like a sack of wet sand and made me see a variety of fireworks before I blacked all the way out.

Chapter 4

The blackout was only temporary, although when I opened my eyes I couldn't see anything but blackness around me. Which meant that the closet door had been shut. And I knew I'd been out for only a few seconds, because I heard the click of the key in the closet lock as Dr. Satchell turned it from outside.

Sounds reached me through the closet door, and my own returning senses told me what they were. Desk drawers being opened and closed in the den. Thumps as Dr. Satchell placed something on the desk or floor. The pad of footsteps then, leaving the room and returning after an interval. Then a repetition of the retreating and returning footsteps. I counted three such brief journeys out there before it occurred to me in my addled state to take any action myself.

I yelled through the door, 'Hey, Dr. Satchell! Are you nuts?' Not a brilliant question to ask of a man who obviously *was* nuts. I wasn't tracking too well yet. Besides, I was suffering from a king-sized case of chagrin at allowing myself to have been conned by the likes of Dr. Satchell. He didn't answer me, though the sounds of movement outside my door continued.

After several attempts, I stood upright in the dark closet and felt groggily around me with my hands and feet. My feet told me that there were no library books stacked on the floor of the closet as Satchell had claimed. And my searching hands told me that the rest of the closet was quite empty, too, except for Hal Johnson, the demon detective. There wasn't even a doorknob on my side of the door. And the door wouldn't budge, even when I leaned my weight against it.

I cleared my throat and bellowed, 'Dr. Satchell?'

This time he answered me. 'Yes, Mr.

Johnson?' Deceptively mild.

'This is going to cost you a hell of a lot more than a fine! What's the idea of slugging me?'

'I told you I had decided on sterner measures.'

'Knocking me on the head and locking me in a closet is what you call sterner measures?'

'No, no. Merely a necessary precaution. It is essential that I keep you ... ah ... safely incommunicado while I proceed.'

'With what?'

'Sterner measures, Mr. Johnson. Aren't you listening?'

I felt a small bead of ice slide down my backbone. 'What sterner measures?'

'They need not concern you.' He kept silent for a moment. Then, 'I *will* tell you one thing, however, Mr. Johnson. I intend to return your filthy books to the library at once. In fact, that's where I am going right this moment.'

Did that explain his three sallies out of the den — to carry the stolen library books out to his car preparatory to returning them to the library? I could hear faint movement through the door before his voice came again. It was high, and thready with excitement. 'Well, goodbye, Mr. Johnson.'

'Wait!' I yelled. 'How's about me? When will you let me out of here?'

'In exactly fifteen minutes,' said Dr. Satchell. 'You must try to be patient until then.' And surprisingly, he laughed. A low snickering kind of laugh that chilled me somehow.

And another bead of ice slowly slid down my spine. Because it suddenly occurred to me that if he was driving to the library or any of its branches to return the stolen books as advertised, he couldn't possibly be back home again in fifteen minutes to release me from the closet. Not even if he used a helicopter. And that funny laugh . . .

I decided not to be patient for fifteen minutes as advised. I decided I had to get out of that closet now. I shouted assorted threats and cajolery through the door at Satchell for several precious minutes without result. Then I shut up and listened. I heard a car start up at the rear of the house and scatter driveway gravel as it rolled out to the street. Satchell had departed. I attacked the closet door.

Maybe it was a thin door with an old rusty lock; maybe anger lent me extra strength; and maybe I was just scared stiff-legged. Whatever it was, my first kick at the door, in the region where the lock should be, split the wooden panel from top to bottom, ripped the lock tongue loose from the splintered door jamb, and catapulted me feet first into the den, where I brought up against Satchell's satinwood desk edge with a rib-shaking jar.

I paused an instant to rub my bruises and catch my breath before launching myself in eager pursuit of Dr. Amos Satchell. And that instant was long enough for me to take startled note of a curious object on Satchell's desk.

In the circumstances it seemed very curious to me. For there, lying beside the onyx ashtray Satchell must have used on my head, was a bright-jacketed copy of that dirty book to end all dirty books

— *The Parallel Triangle*. I was sure it hadn't been there before I entered the closet.

It was one of the library's stolen copies. The library's identification was plainly discernible on cover and spine. Yet for a frozen moment, the significance of its presence there on Satchell's desktop eluded me. I reached out automatically to pick it up. Then, as though arrested in midair by an invisible barrier, my reaching hand stopped dead. And I knew with sickening certainty what Dr. Satchell had meant when he spoke of 'sterner measures'.

The Parallel Triangle was ticking.

Fifteen minutes, Satchell had said. *I'll let you out in fifteen minutes, Mr. Johnson*. Oh yes, he'd let me out all right. By blowing his damned house down around my ears and killing me in the process. Very simple.

How many minutes were left of the promised fifteen? Not many, certainly. I'd dawdled for a good while in the closet before kicking my way out. And I'd dawdled away more precious time right here by this desk.

Besides, what if Satchell had been lying about the fifteen-minute leeway? He'd lied about everything else, so why not? Maybe *The Parallel Triangle* would blow sky-high if I so much as touched it. Maybe Satchell had *counted* on my getting out of his rickety closet and seizing the book.

I shuddered, trying hard to keep myself from panicking. I can admit without shame that I've always been a practicing coward when it comes to explosives of any kind. And I'm all thumbs when it comes to anything electrical. So I didn't even consider trying to disarm Satchell's book-bomb. After all, he was an expert, an ex-professor of electrical engineering or something of the sort. I wasn't about to mess with his ticking bomb.

But I had to do something. A terrifying picture flashed into my mind and stayed there — a picture of Ellen Crosby, my possible future bride, being blown into gory bits when Dr. Amos Satchell returned his stolen books to the library. He wouldn't return them, of course, to the proper check-in desk; no, in all probability, if he returned them at all, he'd slip them quietly onto secluded library shelves where no one would hear them ticking until far too late to avert disaster.

He wouldn't overlook the branch libraries, either, I was pretty sure. After all, he had a whole car-load of book-bombs to work with if he'd gimmicked every copy he'd stolen of those three novels.

So not only my Ellen, but all our librarians, our entire staff, and a lot of innocent men, women and children who would happen to be in the building when the books exploded, were probably in deadly danger, too.

The Parallel Triangle went on ticking merrily away, preventing me from thinking in my usual cool, logical, brilliant fashion. All I could think of to do at that moment was to grab the telephone sitting jauntily beside the book-bomb on Satchell's desktop, dial the police emergency number with a trembling forefinger, and pray a lot. I had Lieutenant Randall, my old boss at the Detective Bureau, on the line in thirty seconds. It seemed like thirty minutes with that ticking in my ears.

Randall said, 'Yeah?' in his bland, bored voice.

'This is Hal Johnson,' I said rapidly, 'and I have only a minute or so to live, so don't interrupt me, for God's sake!' I jerked out my story to him in the fastest briefing anyone ever got, and when he snapped, 'Okay, Hal, I got it,' I hung up the receiver very, very delicately to avoid jarring the ticking book nearby, and then took to my heels as though all the devils in hell were after me.

Chapter 5

I made a new sprint record getting through the front door of Satchell's house and down that long path of stepping stones to the street where my car still stood at the curb. I jumped in, fired up the engine, made a U-turn and started south on City Line Avenue, heading for the main library.

It was not only closer to Satchell's house than any of the branch libraries, but I was confident he'd want to blow it up first anyway, it being, you might say, the main offender in purveying dirty books to the public. I hadn't covered half a block when I heard above the sound of my racing motor a kind of dull thumping boom behind me.

It took me twelve minutes to get downtown, even at my illegal rate of speed. I screeched to a stop beside an unmarked car parked in the no-parking zone directly in front of the main library's entrance. I could see Lieutenant Randall sitting behind the wheel of this unmarked car, talking into a hand mike. I got out of my car, ran around behind it and stuck my head in the open window of Randall's command car and said, 'Well?'

I must have looked and sounded somewhat tense, because Randall switched off and grinned at me. 'Calm down, Junior. Everything's under control.' He glanced complacently at the library. 'We made it in nine minutes flat. That's not bad for a police department that gets more criticism than the president, is it?'

'Has Satchell showed yet?' I stuttered.

'Not yet. Not a sign of him. I've got a man stationed at the entrance of every branch library, just like you wanted. With instructions to hold any white-haired cat in rimless glasses carrying a briefcase or a copy of any of those 'dirty books' you mentioned. Also, I've got a man at every entrance to the main library here with ditto instructions. And I've got another man in a squad car within sight of each door guard to call it in when your nut shows, so I'll know it quick. Relax — wherever he goes, we've got him.' He looked at me narrowly. 'You sure you're not just imagining all this? I notice you weren't blown up in the nut's house, after all.'

'The bomb blew a minute after I left, Lieutenant. I heard it.' I asked anxiously, 'Couldn't you get the libraries evacuated?' I was still picturing Ellen in little pieces.

'Not enough time, Hal. It was goddam miracle just to do what we've done!

Besides, if your crazy friend shows up and finds a bomb scare going on, he's going to back off and come back with his bombs some other day when we're not ready for him. This way, we nail him now.' He looked at his watch again. 'He hasn't shown up yet, Hal. I'm sure of it.'

'But he left his house more than twenty minutes ago! He could've got inside before your men were deployed.'

'No way. How long did it take you drive here from his house?'

'About twelve minutes.'

'See? Satchell wouldn't have made it in less than twenty. He'd drive slow and careful with a carload of bombs, right? And he'd drive by way of the quiet park instead of by that traffic madhouse, City Line Avenue. Right?' I nodded doubtfully. 'And he'll have to find a place to park, which is a fifteen-minute project around any library unless you're lucky. Right? So relax. We've got him, I tell you.'

I was only half-convinced.

'How about the bomb expert?' Lieutenant Randall jerked a thumb over his shoulder. 'Back there,' he said. 'Sergeant

Kwalik, bomb squad.'

I hadn't even noticed the cop in the back seat. I said, 'Hi, Sergeant,' and looked up the broad flight of steps to the main entrance of the library. A plain-clothes detective named Corrigan was standing beside the door up there, keeping a sharp eye out — I hoped — for white-haired men with rimless glasses, briefcases and dirty books.

I had a sudden hunch. I said to Randall, 'Listen, when this nut stole a book from this library yesterday, he left through the technology department exit on the back street. Maybe he'll go in that way now.'

'I've got a man there, I told you. *Every* entrance. Shut up and let me listen to this.' A subdued muttering came over the police band on his radio. 'He hasn't shown up anywhere yet,' he reported then.

I was too antsy to stay there doing nothing. I said, 'I'm going around back and check that technology entrance. Okay?'

Randall was talking into his mike again.

He nodded to me. I ran up the front steps of the library, tipped a hand in greeting to Corrigan as I went through the door, then walked at a more sedate pace through the main library room past Ellen's desk, giving her a big smile as I passed. She returned the smile, not suspecting a thing.

I was enormously relieved to see her once again all in one beautiful piece, even if it might be the last time. I gave the library and reading room a hurried scrutiny as I sailed through them. No sign of Satchell. I was tempted to stop and look in the stacks, but my hunch was still driving me.

I went down the corridor to the technology department on the run. I didn't waste time casing the narrow aisles between bookshelves there, either, but went straight to Laura on the desk. I asked her as casually as I could whether her retired professor friend, Dr. Amos Satchell, had been in today. She said no, looking puzzled.

Without stopping to allay her curiosity, I stepped through the rear door by which

Satchell had exited yesterday and found Pete Calloway, an old friend from my days with the police department, standing guard outside.

I said, 'Hi, Pete. Any action yet?'

'Nothing,' said Pete.

'Nobody came in this way since you've been here?'

'One guy is all. No white hair, though. No briefcase. No rimless glasses. And no dirty books. I looked at them all.'

'He was carrying books?'

'Sure. Six of them. Not the ones we want, though.'

'You sure you looked at them all?' I felt uneasy suddenly.

Pete was hurt. 'Hell yes, Hal. One at a time.'

'Just the covers?'

Pete stared at me. 'What else? I wasn't told to read them all the way through, for God's sake.'

I discovered I was having trouble breathing. I said, 'What color *was* this guy's hair?'

'Brown.'

'And no glasses? Think about it, Pete.'

'No glasses.' Pete was positive. Then he gave me a startled look. 'He blinked a hell of a lot, though,' he said slowly.

I sucked in a deep breath and let it out again. 'How long ago did this guy go in?'

'Couple of minutes. You must have passed him as you came out.'

'I didn't. But he's got to be Satchell, Pete. The nut we're after. Even if he's nutty, this guy isn't stupid. The librarians here know him; he comes in all the time. And he knows we're on to him for stealing books. So he takes off his cheaters and wears a brown wig to disguise himself. And he disguises his dirty books, too.'

'How?'

'Easy. With dust jackets from other library books. Make sense?'

'Could be,' said Pete. He shrugged, then waved both arms over his head.

'What's that for?'

'Signal. It'll bring the lieutenant here on the run with Kwalik.'

'Good,' I said. I was thinking frantically, trying to push down my first impulse, which was to rush into the library and yell for everybody to get out of the building instantly, especially Ellen. Which would no doubt cause a first-class panic. And we didn't want panic now.

What we wanted was Satchell and his armload of books. If Pete's guy *was* Satchell, he'd been inside the library for less than two minutes. Had he seen me, perhaps, and ducked behind something as I went by him? I doubted it. He was probably already out of sight in the stacks of the main library when I came through it.

Because if he meant to deploy most of his six bombs in the main library, which seemed reasonable, he'd have gone directly there to start planting them. Especially if he meant to retreat through the technology department exit after his bombs were planted.

Now then, it would take a minute or two to arm each bomb before he left it on a shelf, wouldn't it? I hoped so. And Satchell would set the triggering mechanism far enough ahead so he'd have plenty of time to get safely out of the library himself before the first bomb exploded. Say ten or fifteen minutes altogether before he finished the job.

I said to Pete, 'Stay here until Randall and Kwalik arrive, will you? Then bring them into the main library stacks. I'll go ahead now and try to locate Satchell. And when you come into the main room, keep it quiet and calm. This guy is crazy enough to blow his whole batch of bombs at once if he sees we're after him. Okay?'

'Okay.'

I went at a quick walking pace through technology, then at a run down the corridor to the main library room. There I slowed and turned into the stacks. At the end of each long, narrow book-lined aisle, I paused just long enough to see whether or not there was a brown-wigged, blinking Dr. Satchell in it anywhere before I went on to inspect the next aisle. Luckily I'm pretty tall. I could see over the heads of most of the people browsing in the stacks who might be blocking out my view of my quarry.

At the fifth aisle, I found him.

Chapter 6

He was alone in the aisle, standing perhaps twenty feet away with his back to me, his head bent over a book that was open in his hand. I drew back a couple of aisles, out of his sight if he turned. I was just in time to flag down Randall, Pete and Kwalik as they came quietly into the stacks. I made shushing signs at them. Randall nodded and raised his eyebrows, asking silently if I'd located Satchell.

I didn't say anything until they were beside me, hidden from Satchell by several aisles of head-high bookshelves. Then I pointed and whispered, 'Twenty feet up aisle number five. Setting the timing gimmick on one of his book-bombs. I didn't see the others.'

That's all Lieutenant Randall needed. Even speaking in a whisper, his command voice came through. 'Go to the other end of that aisle, Hal, around the other cross aisle. Block him there. We'll go in from this end. Kwalik, you go for the bombs. Pete and I will take care of Satchell. When we've got him safe, Kwalik, disarm the bomb he's placing in that aisle. Ready?'

'Wait!' I whispered urgently. 'Suppose he's already planted other bombs on some of these other shelves? We've got to know if and where before we take him. Because he sure as hell won't tell us afterward.'

'How loud do the damn things tick?' Randall growled, momentarily at a loss.

'Not loud enough for Kwalik to find them quick among all these other books!'

Kwalik said, 'How many books was the guy carrying?'

'Six,' Pete said.

'That's it, then,' said Randall, relieved. 'Before we take Satchell, we locate and count the books he's still got with him. If he has five left, we know he's only planted the one so far. And Hal knows where that one is. All right? Let's go.'

I walked to the far end of aisle one, where we'd been standing, found the cross-aisle, leading to aisle five, empty, and cautiously took my position just around the corner of aisle five in the cross-aisle. I peered through the gaps in the bookshelves between us and saw

Satchell closing the cover of the book in his hand very carefully.

From where I was, I couldn't see what he'd done with his other books. He pushed the books on a middle shelf beside him tightly together, to make room for another book. Then he slid his armed bomb into the opening thus made, and turned away from me toward the other end of the aisle.

I risked a peek around my corner. Randall and his men were coming slowly down aisle five from the other end; Kwalik, the bomb expert, in the lead. Craning around my corner, I saw why Kwalik was leading instead of Randall. On the floor by Satchell's feet was a little pile of books with bright covers. I counted them with my heart in my throat. Five.

Satchell was beginning to stoop to pick them up when Kwalik reached him. The timing couldn't have been better. Satchell, thinking Kwalik was just another library patron browsing through the stacks, turned slightly sideways to allow him to pass him in the narrow aisle.

Kwalik didn't pass him. 'Excuse me, sir,' he said to Satchell in a polite, help-the-old-lady-across-the-street voice, 'can't I help you with these?' He half-knelt at Satchell's feet, and with a smooth, unhurried, sweeping movement of practiced hands, scooped up Satchell's five remaining book-bombs and backed quickly away on his knees, allowing Randall and Pete to pass him in the aisle and bracket a bewildered Satchell neatly between them.

By this time, I was approaching the huddle of figures from my end of the aisle. I saw the quick glint of metal and heard the clicks that told me Randall and Pete had each handcuffed himself to one of Satchell's wrists.

Poor Satchell couldn't go anywhere now without dragging two burly cops with him. Amazingly, Satchell still used the low tone of voice that old library custom demands when he said to Lieutenant Randall, 'What do you think you're doing, may I ask?'

I didn't hear what Randall answered, if anything. I was watching Kwalik, the bomb boy, with those chills running up and down my spine again.

Kwalik cleared a space on a handy shelf behind him and gently placed Satchell's five books on it, flat side down. Then, with his fingertips, he delicately lifted the cover of one of the books a fraction of an inch, held it there with one hand, got out a pencil flashlight with the other, and shone the light into the crack. He peered inside, his head tilted slightly. He looked as though he was ready to run. I know I was.

At length Kwalik nodded to Randall. 'Okay,' he said, 'these'll wait. Where's the live one?'

I said, 'Here it is, Sergeant.' I bent over and put my ear to the book Satchell had slipped in among the others on that middle shelf. And by God, it was ticking! Up to that moment, I hadn't quite been able to believe that Satchell really intended to wipe out five buildings full of books and people. Six buildings, if you counted his own house with me in it. But that ticking book made a true believer out of me. 'Hurry up, Sergeant!' I said to

Kwalik, and backed off like a timid schoolgirl to the end of the aisle. Have I mentioned that I'm scared of explosives?

Kwalik had nerves of ice, apparently. He removed the ticking book from the shelf, opened its cover and disengaged, with a touch like a jeweler's, a wire somewhere inside the hollowed-out book. 'Got it,' he said calmly. Then, to Pete, 'You sure he only had six books when he came in?'

'I'm sure,' Pete said. 'I may be dumb but I can at least *count*!' He was disgusted with himself for letting Satchell get by him at the door.

Satchell himself hadn't said a word since his first weak protest to Randall. Probably because he couldn't believe his eyes when he saw me coming down the corridor toward him. He thought I was dead. His face had paled and his reddish-brown eyes, a nice match for his brown wig, now contained more desperation than they had yesterday — and more resignation, too.

Randall said, 'Pick up your goddam 'dirty books', Kwalik, and let's get the hell out of here. I never have felt comfortable in a library!' He turned to me. 'I don't suppose you know what kind of car the professor here drives? So we can collect the rest of his books?'

'Sorry, I never saw his car.'

Surprisingly, Dr. Satchell spoke up then. He said meekly, 'The rest of the bombs are in my blue Ford sedan, parked on the street behind the library.' He gave Lieutenant Randall the license number. Randall jerked on his handcuff and growled, 'Show us where.'

I followed them out of the stacks, down the corridor to technology, through technology to the rear exit. It was a regular parade. Kwalik went first with his armload of deadly books. Then came Randall, Satchell and Pete, shoulder to shoulder like old buddies, handcuffs hidden under jacket cuffs. Then me, bringing up the rear, lagging as far behind those bombs in Kwalik's arms as I respectably could. Laura, on the technology desk, scarcely lifted her head from her book as we went by.

I looked at my watch. Incredibly, from

the moment I'd first realized that Satchell might be inside the library till now, when he and his bomb-books were leaving it under guard, only four and a half minutes had elapsed. They were four and a half of the longest minutes I could remember.

Yet I knew I'd gladly go through a dozen more like them — or a hundred — to keep Ellen Crosby in one piece. Even if she decided *not* to marry me. Girls with faces like Botticelli angels and figures like Egyptian belly-dancers aren't all that easy to find these days. You know what I mean?

We do hope that you have enjoyed reading this large print book.

Did you know that all of our titles are available for purchase?

We publish a wide range of high quality large print books including:
**Romances, Mysteries, Classics
General Fiction
Non Fiction and Westerns**

Special interest titles available in large print are:
**The Little Oxford Dictionary
Music Book, Song Book
Hymn Book, Service Book**

Also available from us courtesy of Oxford University Press:
**Young Readers' Dictionary
(large print edition)
Young Readers' Thesaurus
(large print edition)**

For further information or a free brochure, please contact us at:
**Ulverscroft Large Print Books Ltd.,
The Green, Bradgate Road, Anstey,
Leicester, LE7 7FU, England.
Tel:** (00 44) **0116 236 4325
Fax:** (00 44) **0116 234 0205**

THE WHISPERING WOMAN

Gerald Verner

Paula Rivers, a beautiful, haughty young cinema cashier, is selling tickets when her sister Eileen delivers a portentous note to her: *'Be careful. People who play with fire get badly burned. Sometimes they die.'* Not long afterward, Paula is found murdered in her booth, shot from behind. Who was the haggard old woman dressed in black who had accosted Eileen and told her to give Paula the note? Called to investigate, Superintendent Budd is faced with one of the most curious mysteries of his career.

MURDER FORETOLD

Denis Hughes

Agent John Bentick is not enjoying his latest assignment for British Intelligence — personal bodyguard to Nargan, an abrasive foreign diplomat on a covert mission to exchange military secrets. On their arrival at the isolated house of Professor Dale in Cornwall, Bentick senses an atmosphere of mystery and menace generated by Dale's latest invention — a sinister machine that is somehow shaping the destiny of everyone in the house. Soon he finds himself a helpless pawn in a figurative chess game that can only end in death . . .

THE OTHER MRS. WATSON'S CASEBOOK

Michael Mallory

The indomitable Amelia Watson, second wife of the famous doctor, continues to bend her formidable intellect to solving further crimes. Whether foiling anarchists, investigating a possible murder committed high above the streets of London, rescuing her old theatre colleague Harry Benbow from a decidedly awkward scrape involving a haunted house, untangling the connection behind a trail of all-too-real headless corpses, or determining the truth behind a case of apparent spontaneous combustion, this respectable Edwardian lady remains a force to be reckoned with.

VICTIMS OF EVIL

Victor Rousseau

A gang led by the mysterious Doctor
Omega is targeting prominent New
York financiers for blackmail. One
victim arranges a police trap for the
criminals — which fails. Revenge is
swift and brutal. The defiant financier
is assaulted by an unseen hand in a
peculiar and gruesome manner, left
unconscious and bleeding from his left
eye. When he wakes, the full horror of
the attack becomes apparent. For the
man is still alive, but left babbling
gibberish and unable to communi-
cate . . .